A WARRIORS OF MAIDA NOVELLA

LOVE *Me* TENDER

Award Winning Author
RENEE FIELD

Love Me Tender

A Warriors of Maida Novella, Volume 2

Renee Field

Published by Renee Field, 2015.

Love Me Tender
A Warriors Maida Novella, 2

By Renee Field

Novella previously published by Ellora's Cave

Chapter One

"I told you that I like them feisty," snarled Tyrana. She eyed the four men lying on the plush red velvet pillows that encompassed the pleasure room. "Do they look feisty to you?"

"I told you before, Tyrana, none of them are feisty. We can't even make them pretend to behave that way. What do you want me to do?" asked Sarah, with an exaggerated sigh of frustration.

Sarah was her most trusted friend. She engaged in all of Tyrana's wicked sexual romps, but none of it was fun anymore. None of it held any meaning to her. She had *rutted* with close to a hundred Maida men, only once though. That was her cardinal rule that she held firm to. Not that it mattered anymore.

Her life felt empty, without purpose, and she was weary to death of it all.

Learning that her sister, Rowena, was fertile had left her feeling hollow. It was as if her very own little sister had kicked her in the gut. The white-hot envy that had sprung to the surface scared Tyrana. *Why her?* It was a thought she couldn't discard.

Why is it my sister, the favorite one, the self-described workaholic, is the one who ends up fertile? That question circled in Tyrana's mind like a repeating loop, making her feel slightly ill.

A loud groan from one of the men caused Tyrana to turn her attention back to the four men. All of the men were either stroking their shafts to entice her gaze or rubbing their stones. She rolled her eyes. Bored at the very sight, she turned and sauntered out of the room.

"You're not going to fuck them?" asked Sarah, clearly amazed Tyrana had, for once, passed up the chance to fornicate.

In truth, so was she. *Why bother. Why, by the Saints, should I when it no longer pleasures me. Maybe I'm coming down with that Castima flu.* Tyrana tried hard to ascribe her strange feelings to something.

1

Anything was better than realizing the lure of sex had lost its appeal to her.

Her sister would have laughed at that one. Sex no longer brought her the temporary relief she longed for. Striding down the long corridor, she vowed to stop her little self-pity act.

What exactly is the purpose of my life? It was a question she asked herself for the umpteenth time that day. It was a day like any other. The sun shone brightly. The sky was as blue and crystal clear as the still waters that surrounded All Saints Lake, but Tyrana felt unsettled. She yearned to lash out at something...anything, but she couldn't.

"Just where do you think you're going?" asked her mother, stepping out into the corridor.

Her mother wore the long, purple traditional Council robe, reminding Tyrana that her mother was Her Majesty, ruler of the Supreme High Fertility Council. It was a slap in the face that she'd never be offered a seat because, yet again, she didn't measure up.

Brushing past her mother, she mouthed the word, "Out."

"No, you are not. This is for you," said her mother, handing her an envelope that had her name embossed in a bold fancy gold script.

When Tyrana made no move to take it, her mother tried another tactic.

"It's from your sister. Be courteous, take it, read it and write to her," she demanded, attempting to forcibly open Tyrana's hand.

"I'm not interested," she replied, letting the yellow-stained envelope fall like a rose petal to the floor. She resisted the urge to stomp on it. That would be too childish. She walked away as her mother swept down, picked up the envelope and gathered her flowing robe around her in a huff, but not before jabbing her with her usual parting words.

"Why can't you be *good* for once, like your sister?" she snapped, opening the Council Chamber door to disappear inside.

There it was again. That *good* word. Tyrana had long ago taken *that* word out of her vocabulary. It had never fit her. It was never what the Blessed Mother Saint had in mind for her.

So the word *good* had been ditched and replaced with wicked, bad and naughty. Those were the words people used to describe her. Those were the words of comfort that kept her warm, cocooned like a fluffy blanket in the dark of the night. After all, on Maida, if you didn't get the curse and become fertile, you weren't "good" enough.

The funny thing was, she had always assumed that it would be Rowena, her science loving sister who would end up infertile—not her. But that was the crux of the problem facing all Maida women. The fertility curse chose women randomly.

The choice of motherhood wasn't theirs. It had been taken away from them a long time ago by the men who had almost destroyed their world. It had been their radioactive weapons that had released the poisonous ions into the atmosphere, into the water, into the soil and, worse, into their genetic DNA —the material that made them what they were. Those were the words her sister spoke in passion. All Tyrana had cared about at one time in her life was pleasing her mother, having a child of her own and taking a seat on the Supreme High Fertility Council.

She huffed loudly. *Not anymore.* That dream had dissipated over five years ago when she finally mustered the courage to take the fertility test. There had always been a part of her that had held out hope over the accumulation of years that eventually she'd be hit with the curse. Turning twenty-eight years of age had been her awakening. Even though many Maida women went through the curse late in life, Tyrana knew on that blessed day that marked her birth that it wasn't going to happen to her. To finally put an end to that kernel of hope, she'd undertaken the test. The red stain of the liquid inside the test tube had told her what her heart dreaded. She was infertile.

From that moment on, her life had changed. Her dreams had ended. She'd learned to live day to day, not expecting much. The devastation and keen knowledge that she was barren, that her womb would never nourish a baby, was a deep ache within her, which she kept to herself.

She wished she could have confided in her sister, but she hadn't. Instead, she let the years wash by them, moving them emotionally further away from each other. At one time, she and Rowena had shared every secret together. But all that changed when Tyrana learned she was the infertile one. And then her sister became wrapped up in her own passion to find a cure for the fertility curse. Tyrana laughed. She had never viewed fertility as the dreadful curse. What was worse was being infertile, barren and unable to procreate to further the Maida race.

Knowing that her sister was about to be married and had probably already conceived a child carved a deep wide gulf through Tyrana's heart. *That baby should have been mine. Rowena never wanted a baby.* Tyrana couldn't cope with seeing Rowena at the moment. It was just too much to bear. That was why Tyrana ignored her sister's letters.

Tyrana shook her head, clearing the useless emotional thoughts that threatened her control. With no destination in mind, she strode out the palace doors and walked across the well-manicured, vibrant green lawn. Looking back at the palace that was her childhood home, she was hit with a realization—she hated everything about it.

It was a sterile environment that had become her own prison—filled with no expectations of what she could do with her life, except live irresponsibly. It was a trap she felt she'd never escape from. Her heart thundered with that realization. Her sister would think she, Tyrana, known as the infertile one, had more freedom than her. Sadly, that wasn't the case. *There is no freedom when choice is taken from you.*

Deep in thought, she continued to walk briskly away from the palace. A shout from behind stilled her.

"Get back! Get back! Look out!" shouted a Maida guard just as a man ran at lightning speed past her, almost toppling her to the ground.

Tyrana twirled around to maintain her balance. She saw out of the corner of her eye that the man had turned almost in slow motion to watch her. Then the guard grasped her arm.

"Get back, he's not safe," said the guard.

But Tyrana didn't care what the guard had to say. She was interested in the man who had the nerve to grin mischievously at her and the audacity to boldly wink at her. *What is he thinking?*

What am I thinking? She studied his physique quickly, her eyes drawn to his mid-waist in the half a minute it took for him to run straight into the Dark Forest. He was at least two heads taller than her. He was broad of shoulder, with straight rust-colored hair that fell to his mid-back, a back that rippled with muscles gleaming from the high noon sun. And his ass. By the Saints, it had her salivating on the spot. Her pussy juices started to flow just with the image of his long shaft she had eyed with longing as he raced past her naked as the day he was born. Thoughts of his coppery, molten-looking skin left her feeling a hunger she couldn't describe.

"He's the man who's been dropping off your sister's letters. Your mother told us to capture him for more information as to her whereabouts. So far, we've had no luck. And there is no way I'm going into the Dark Forest," said the Maida guardswoman, finally releasing her hold on Tyrana's arm.

"He's too fast for us, but what a chase," she cackled. "Nothing like running in the hot noon sun with that ass in front of you."

Again the guard chortled, trying to get Tyrana to share in the joke about the man's ass gleaming in the sun. However, Tyrana was in no mood to play nice, especially if that meant sharing anything at all that had to do with the man who had sparked an intense heat in her throbbing core.

Then what the guardswoman said penetrated Tyrana's brain. *This man, this oh-so yummy want to fuck me 'til I die man, has been in contact with my sister.* By the Saints, Tyrana wanted him and meant to have him.

Brushing off the guardswoman, Tyrana strode forward for once taking her own future into her hands. While the warnings from the guardswoman were loud, Tyrana ignored them.

After all, she had heard them all before. Anyone who entered the Dark Forest never came out. Well, that myth was no longer true. Her sister had ventured into the forest and fallen in love with a man she was about to marry.

Then it will be babies and all that stuff. Tyrana hated that jealous ache that pitted itself deep within her when she thought of the life her sister got to live. It was a life she would never know. It was a part of being a woman she'd never discover.

It's a burden anyway, she told herself, wishing that the yearning to have a baby of her own flesh would leave her. That desire was like a scab that painfully itched and blistered under her skin.

But here, Tyrana thought, was the perfect distraction—that man! A daring plan formed in her mind. She would track that man who knew where her sister was for her own purposes. She wanted him.

A fever the likes of which she had never experienced before caused her body to flush with desire simply thinking about that fine specimen of a man who had gamely winked at her. She wanted...no, *needed* to have that cock of his lodged deep within her wet pussy. *Maybe if I fuck long and hard enough, I'll forget about everything else.*

That's it! This man will be my cure. Just the thought of that feisty all-too-male coppery body at her beck and call, on his knees in front of her, caused her to grin in sweet anticipation. Tyrana vowed to all the Saints that she would get what she wanted this time, no matter what.

Chapter Two

Rusty planned on killing his best friend, Tulon, the minute he got back to the Plains. To think he had actually agreed for the second time to deliver a message for his friend's mate, Rowena, caused all the hairs on his skin to bristle. *Stupid! Naive!* He wanted to hit something.

The Maida women were bizarre and some of them were downright scary. Twice now, the woman warriors had tried to capture him. *I don't think so.*

He was a Mage Pegcentaur, capable of wielding magic far beyond their understanding. However, he couldn't ignore the fact that he found the chase highly sporting. And today his eyes had been richly rewarded when he spied the most alluring Maida woman yet. She walked with a regal bearing and he was pleased to note that her head would come to rest just below his chin. He had always liked his women tall, but most females of his kind tended to be too short for his liking.

She had long wavy chestnut hair streaked with a hint of red. And she had full high breasts, clad in a tight leather top that had fired his shaft to attention. Most of all, he liked that when he had gamely winked at her, she had notched up her chin in defiance and squared her shoulders against the shock of it. Without a doubt, he knew she was going to come after him.

The idea had him more aroused than he had been in a long time. Delivering messages for Rowena at least gave him something new to do. That was the crux of things. Rusty was mighty bored with life. Nothing seemed to matter to him. And he was sick and tired of being in charge of all the blasted *younglings*, the wannabe Mage Pegcentaur warriors who continually drove him nuts with their whining.

He had never asked to be head of the warrior clan. It had simply been assumed he'd fall into the role because his father had led them for centuries. That had never sat well with Rusty. In fact, he had tried to refuse, but the Mage Council refused to listen to him. *How infuriating!*

What he really wanted was simplicity—not that he would ever tell anyone, let alone Tulon, that. Being a warrior had long ago lost its appeal, but the love of the land held him enthralled and that too he kept to himself.

So now the chance to play, to have some fun with this Maida woman, engulfed all of his senses. He caught her scent the moment she stepped into the Dark Forest. In a flash, he transformed into a stallion, knowing if she spotted him as a horse, she'd be anything but afraid. *And afraid she most certainly should be.* He grinned, thinking of all the wonderfully wicked things he planned to do to the curious woman. Didn't she know that curiosity sparked the flame? And his was just aching for a breath of fresh air.

The crunch of leaves underfoot was the only sound echoing in the stillness of the forest. The blanket of thick tall trees made it appear dusk-like to Tyrana's eyes, but still it didn't deter her. Relying on her skills as a tracker, which all Maida women learned during their teenage years, wasn't much comfort but it would suffice. She turned right, groping her way around a large boulder that looked as if it had been thrown in the middle of the forest. There, before her startled eyes, was a sight.

As if it didn't have a care in the world, a large copper-brown stallion with a thick red mane stood staring at her, almost daring her to move forward. Tyrana moved forward slightly awed at the sheer wild presence of the majestic creature.

"Aren't you a beauty, my handsome steed. Did you by chance see a naked man run through here?" Tyrana laughed. *Half an hour into the Dark Forest and I'm already talking to myself. That's not good.*

When the stallion snorted and pawed the ground, she could have sworn it was beckoning her to come closer. When it pawed at the ground again with its right hoof, she knew without a doubt it was demanding her presence.

"Look, my lovely, I can't stay. I'm hunting myself a man," she said, cautiously moving closer so she could stroke its velvety smooth side. It was then she noticed why he was pawing the ground. High on his right leg was a large bite and it was bleeding. The horse was in need of help.

Without thought, Tyrana tore a large piece of fabric from her knee-length skirt. "Now, I won't hurt you, but you've got to stay still." Slowly, she bent and wrapped the torn fabric tightly around the horse's hind leg. Task completed, she stood and smiled, pleased with her mediocre doctoring skills when the steady stream of blood ceased.

Patting the stallion's velvety side, she all but crooned at it. "There now, you rest here and everything will be all right."

The horse's eyes were the color of light green grass and his mane was luxuriously thick with flecks of gold highlighting the ends. He vibrated with life and there was a wild edge to his eyes, informing her no one was going to tame this beast. That thought brought Tyrana comfort. He was too magnificent. Too wild. She hoped he never ventured from the Dark Forest into Maida lands.

When she was finally able to compose herself and walk away from the magnificent creature, he followed her. *This isn't going to do at all.*

"You need to stay here." This time her voice was firm and commanding.

When the stallion shook its head at her and snorted, she almost stamped her foot. "Fine, suit yourself, but don't get in my way. That man's mine."

Great, just great. I'm left talking to a horse about a man...life just couldn't get any better now, could it? She turned and marched forward through the dense thicket, not once bothering to look back, even as the underbrush grew denser.

By nightfall, she'd had it. She was exhausted, sweaty, cranky, hungry and completely bewildered. All day she thought she'd been tracking the man, only it had turned out to be a hare. *A bloody bunny.* She fumed at her own stupidity.

Aching to simply give up, that was no longer a possibility. She had ventured so far into the Dark Forest that, for the love of the Saints, Tyrana had no idea which way was home. Not that she had any intention of giving up or going home.

Tyrana forced herself to gather evergreens to make a comfortable bed on the hard earth. A shiver racked through her body. *What I wouldn't give for a fire or even a roasted bunny.* A slightly terrified giggle escaped her.

A blanket would be good about now. She tried again to glimpse the stars through the cloudy expanse of dark sky that every once in a while peeked its way through the canopy of towering trees. Tucking her shivering body under a large tree, a low rumbling whinny alerted her that the stallion who had been following her all day was still with her.

"Go make your own bed," she snapped, annoyed with herself that she felt pleased by its presence.

When it stomped at the ground and huffed at her, she glared back at it.

"And don't you dare tell me you're lost too." Tyrana's voice echoed in the stillness of the night. This time when he snorted, it wasn't one of pleasure. In fact, the stallion looked none too pleased with her as its green eyes glared at her.

She couldn't help but shiver from his gaze. Turning her body more into the cold comfort of the tree, she tucked about a dozen evergreen boughs around her body—anything for comfort. Her last thought as her eyes closed from exhaustion was just what, by the Saints, had she gotten herself into.

Chapter Three

Rusty couldn't believe the stupidity of the beautiful Maida woman. *She couldn't track her own backside if she tried.* He snorted, having tried numerous times during the course of the day to turn her back toward Maida territory.

All had been for naught. So intent was she on finding him that she had spurned all of his help. She shivered from the cold. *That woman has never slept a day in her life in the outdoors.* He eyed the covering she was attempting to make to try to keep warm. He all but snorted in disgust.

His entire body longed for the comfort of his home and the Plains. Not these dark woods. His kind rarely ventured far afield—it wasn't in their nature. The journey he had undertaken twice now for Rowena's sake showed him there was a lot more to the world than he had surmised. His leg itched where the snake had bitten him.

Ugh, he hated snakes. And to have an eye-spur asp mark him rankled the warrior he was. Luckily, he had used his Mage magic to stop the poison from leeching through his system. Then he had promptly trampled the deadly snake into the mud. The poison left him momentarily weak. That knowledge didn't sit well with Rusty. But he had been surprised by how tender the actions of the Maida woman were.

She had pleased and surprised him. Even though she was cautious when she approached him, she didn't flinch with fear. Worse was the singe of heat he felt from the contact of her fingers on his skin. Her scent of wild lilies engulfed his senses. It had taken every ounce of willpower he had possessed to force his cock to stay limp while her hands had skillfully administered to his bite.

Still though, she's naive to travel into unknown territory without some sort of power. He knew she had none. No Maida was born with magic. They believed in science, rules and order.

As much as Rusty wanted to taste the little Maida woman, he also wanted her safe and that meant getting her back to Maida territory. *I'd like to teach her a little bit of order. Like how to follow a path straight home.* He sighed, exasperated.

The border of the Dark Forest had kept his kind and theirs separate since long before the first wars. Wars that had ravaged and scorched the planet Alvaron. Even though he hadn't been born then, Rusty knew from the stories told by the Elders that it had taken the combined efforts of some of the most powerful Mages to keep Maida's poisonous weapons out of the Plains. However, there were tell-tale signs by the edge of the Dark Forest that the woods had been infected by their radioactive bombs.

Why the Maida would want to destroy Alvaron mystified him. He had learned a lot from Rowena before agreeing to travel into Maida lands. Some of what she told him shocked his beliefs.

Why would anyone want to imprison another? It wasn't something he could get his head around. He knew Maida women had become leaders after the last great destructive war—a war that nearly crippled the planet. How could they think keeping men as slaves was all right? That's what the men were, no matter how prettily Rowena had tried to make them sound like domestic workers or laborers. Anyone kept from doing what they wanted was a slave...nothing more.

His kind had long ago learned becoming domesticated wasn't within their nature. Rusty highly doubted being told when to eat, sleep and what to do was the inherent nature of Maida men. *Someday, they too will rebel and who will get hurt then?*

Rusty shook his head. None of these questions were getting him anywhere. How he almost wished his friend had never given the gift of creation to Rowena. There were many among his kind who felt Tulon had been wrong. Giving the gift of creation to a creature of non-magic was viewed as an infraction of the rules.

No Maida had ever been granted permission to stay in their lands before, either. Then again, no creature made of magic had ever fallen in love with a Maida woman. Rusty huffed with that notion. Love was something he had no intention of succumbing to. *Lust, well, that's another thing entirely.*

His hands itched to finally discover what a Maida woman truly felt and tasted like. How did it feel to have a Maida woman climax from the intense pleasure he knew he could give? The idea caused the hairs on his skin to tingle with awareness as the Maida woman's frustrated lonely sigh washed over him like a night's kiss.

He watched the woman squirm to find some warmth from the evergreen boughs she had tucked around her. *Hopeless.* She was completely unprepared for the journey she had undertaken, which showed how rash and naive she was. If she thought she'd be able to survive the Dark Forest on her own, she was in for a rude awakening. Thrice he had taken the time to appease the Forest Guardians to ensure they were granted safe passage through their lands. He had no intention of pissing any of them off, knowing full well what the trees in the forest were capable of.

Now, however, time was running out. They were no longer welcome. He had to get her up and out of the forest before the moon rose to its full height or else. He knew all about the consequences, but she was oblivious to their plight. So he flashed into his human form, determined to get her to safety. Eyeing her lush body, he first planned on stoking some of that inner fire of hers he had glimpsed.

Rowena arched her back into the source of heat, letting it engulf her achingly cold limbs. She heaved a sigh of relief. Then she felt two hands roam over her breasts, causing them and her to instantly awaken. Twisting her head around sharply, she found the solid source of heat warming her backside—a man. And not just any man. The blasted man she had been tracking all day.

Not one for small talk when actions spoke louder than words, she promptly unfurled her arms from around her front to his backside, bringing his hard, lean body up close and personal. She heard his "um" of surprise when she squeezed his ass.

He was now clad in velvet brown breeches that molded his round sculpted cheeks to perfection. She loved that he had nothing covering his chest. The intense heat of skin to skin contact caused her to shiver. Thankfully, he didn't speak, but proceeded to pinch her nipples to hardened buds. The pain and pleasure of it swamped her aching pussy. How she longed for his hard, long cock to be jammed tight within her slick opening.

She knew it was long because somehow, in the process of heating her, he had raised her knee-length skirt so her ass was bare to the feel of his engorged cock. Her tiny black thong didn't leave much to the imagination. The combination of the crisp night air and his body heat was a wicked recipe for fueling her desire. She felt him lean into her, letting her get a good feel of his thick, hard shaft and his heavy stones as they bunched together in the tight confines of his breeches. Her breath caught in her throat as the musky wild grassy scent of him sizzled her senses.

When he moved a hand from her breast and slid it between her legs, she parted them on her own, letting him know her need. Tenderly, he slid a hot hand under her thong and through her wet folds, and then boldly plunged a finger deep into her cunt. Her inner muscles clenched around him, begging for more. Before she knew it, he removed his finger.

She twisted her head around and watched him. *The blasted tease.* He took his finger and moved it to his own mouth and sucked her juices off of it. That erotic gesture caused her to squirm with intense need as she jiggled her ass closer to entice him.

"You want it, don't you, my little filly." The man's voice was a deep rumble that vibrated straight to her womb.

She arched more into his body, hoping he'd get the hint. *Why, by the Saints, isn't he putting that cock of his to good use?* The strain of unquenched desire was starting to spill over into sexual frustration—something she had never experienced before.

Maida men were always accommodating. No man had ever teased her like this. And none had ever looked like the man that was cuddling, fondling and playing her like she was a fine instrument about to be tuned. She tried yet again to shake her ass into position so that his cock could slide into her wet folds. *Any wetter and I'll become a puddle of blazing desire.*

Twisting her body around so she was now face to face with him, she all but gasped. He was ruggedly beautiful and all male. So masculine that, for one moment, she forgot to breathe. He looked like a man of legend. His face was large, and while his nose jutted out more than what she had expected, it only served to highlight his other features.

He had a deep rust-colored shadow of a beard highlighting his high cheekbones. His flaming auburn hair was long and tied back from his face. His eyes were a startling shade of green, reminding her of the green moss of the forest floor. They stared at her with such intense heat, she instinctively wet her lips. She watched his reaction to that bold, seductive move.

When he mimicked her actions—his tongue slowly circling his thick lips—it was her turn to blush. A bold wink from him caused her to squirm with unbridled passion.

So the man wants to play. Well, she could be a hellcat if she liked. After all, playing before pouncing did have its merits. Shamelessly, she rubbed her breasts against his naked, muscled chest, wishing she was naked so she could feel the fine dusting of light orange curly hair that covered his chest against her aroused body.

His gaze turned smoldering, bringing the irises of his eyes to a shade of dark green as he watched her work her body onto his. She loved that his chest hairs darkened to a fine line past his navel. That too startled her. He was unlike any Maida man she had ever known and she had known a lot.

Maida men were not allowed to grow beards and none she knew sported chest hair. What she longed for was the feel of his fine chest hairs up against her bare breasts. Too bad she had on her leather halter top.

"Like what you see?" he asked, once again forking out his tongue to lick his lips.

Blast his voice. She shook her head, hating that he could disarm her simply with his voice that plucked and pulled at her wet pussy muscles.

Tilting her chin up to face him, she pulled him tighter to her. "What I'd like is for you to put that cock of yours deep inside of me. Now." She lowered her voice to a seductive whisper.

"Ahh, I had heard Maida women were straight-forward and brazen and methinks I am going to like you a lot. But alas, my little filly, the pleasure of fucking you until you scream from me filling you will have to wait until we are out of this blasted forest."

With that long speech, he promptly moved away from her. He stood up, letting her entire body succumb to the cold night air while providing her with a mighty good look at his entire body.

He was startlingly tall. At least two heads taller than her. Besides being broad of shoulder, he had long thick legs, and she could clearly see the muscle definition outlined from his tight breeches. She could also see the huge bulge that rested between his legs.

Spellbound, she watched as the man reached with his large hands into his breeches to pull out his cock. *By the Saints.* She groaned out loud with longing. Her cunt dripped with a fierce need. He had to have the longest, thickest shaft she had ever seen—and she thought she'd seen it all.

His cock was rigidly beautiful, thick and long and his stones were so full and heavy she wondered if he was in discomfort. Before her eyes, she watched him take his engorged member in one hand while the other cupped his stones. Then he stroked his cock. His eyes were shut with need. It was like she no longer existed. He had forgotten about her and the blasted man was intent on taking his own pleasure without her.

The crude gesture of what he was doing should have mortified her. It didn't. She watched, licking her lips, as he continued to stroke himself, his shaft thickening even more. How that was possible, she didn't know. She had never seen a Maida man with such a thick cock.

She wondered if her small body would be able to accommodate all of him. Then she noticed his eyes had opened and he was watching her reaction.

"Ahh, my little filly, don't even go there. My cock will fit perfectly inside that sweet cunt of yours. I plan to stuff you full of me, until I touch that womb of yours. After I fuck you, you will finally know what it's like to be taken by a real man," he said proudly, still stroking his engorged member.

His words were an erotic promise. Her breasts tingled and her nipples hardened even more. No Maida man had dared to speak to her like that before. She loved it. Her body loved it. And she craved more.

Chapter Four

She watched as he grasped his cock and stroked it faster. *By the Saints, is the blasted man going to climax on his own without me?* Not if she had anything to do with it.

Crawling to her knees, she faced him. There was a moment when he looked down at her and grinned.

"Ahh, you look good on your knees," he said.

Before he could say anything else, she brazenly reached for his shaft and took the wide tip of it into her mouth. She tried to suck hard.

The man pulled out so fast, she knew she looked ridiculous with her mouth puckered like she was a blasted fish.

"By the Heavenly Saints, what are you doing?" he asked, his eyes wide, his stance one clearly of surprise.

Can it be? She frowned. Did he honestly not know what she had been attempting to do? She assumed from his earlier bold moves that he was experienced. Apparently his experiences had never included a blow job before.

Standing and moving to his side, she watched as he took another step back. "I was planning on sucking you off," she said, pleased to note that her words caused his cock to jump back to stand at full attention.

"With your mouth?"

"Yes, with my mouth. How else could I suck you?" Tyrana all but snapped at him. Whether it was his reaction or the cool night air, she no longer felt in the mood. She was cranky, angry and once again cold. She was no longer sure he was the man she wanted. For one, he talked too much. She had always liked her men silent, and this one seemed the chatty type. Plus, she was tired and annoyed at him.

"What's your designation?" she asked, recalling she didn't know where he had come from.

"My designation...if you mean my name, my friends call me Rusty," he said, bowing to her in an old-fashioned gesture as he tucked his member back into his breeches.

Even though he was barefoot, bare chested and clad only in breeches, he pulled off that one bow with grace and elegance, as if he were royalty. *As if.*

"And you are?" he asked, clearly waiting for her to reply.

For a split second, Tyrana thought about telling him her real name, but then she hesitated. If he knew who she was, he'd treat her differently. Of that she had no doubt. "I am Mira," she said, deciding to use one of her many middle names instead.

"Well, Mira, why were you tracking me?" he asked, moving even further away from her.

She blurted out the first thing that came to her mind. "I heard you were the messenger delivering notes from Her Majesty's daughter, Rowena, and I was simply curious."

She hoped he'd buy that lie, because for the love of the blessed Mother Saint, she couldn't think of what else to say.

"Ahh, I see. So you thought to capture me for yourself, didn't you?" he asked, crossing his arms over his chest.

"Well...sort of," she admitted.

"I am not the capturing kind." He cocked his head to the side like he was listening for something. "We need to be on our way." He turned and walked away from her.

The view of his muscular ass was splendid. Two round muscled cheeks that bespoke of power and stamina strained the fabric of his tight breeches. She all but drooled on the spot.

"Once you are done eyeing my ass, get yours moving, because time is running out," he said, ordering her to move her butt.

She reeled. It was one thing to have him be domineering in sex play but it was an entirely different matter when her thoughts were no longer centered on sex.

"I am not going with you," she replied, turning in the opposite direction.

Before she could even squeak a reply, he grabbed her from behind, turning her body so she faced him. He clenched both of her wrists in one of his large hands and forced them behind her back, making it impossible for her to move. Then he pulled her body to his so that her breasts were touching his chest. With his other hand, he grasped her ass, bringing her body close to his bulging member.

The intimate feel of his arousal ignited a need within her like dynamite. As much as she resented his superior strength over her, a part of her roared to life. She dared him to do more. Tossing her long hair out of her eyes, she stood, bracing her feet wide as she tilted her face up to him.

"Ahh, my little filly, you like it rough," he said.

Again she stilled as the silky rumble of his voice like that of a fine wine streamed through her entire body, wetting her core even more. She shook her head to clear her mind.

Then he kissed her. It wasn't a tender kiss. It was a kiss that marked her. She fought not to open her lips but that was futile. He nipped and bit at her lower lip, and when she took a breath of air for her burning lungs, he plunged his tongue inside of her, forcing her to comply. The entire time he kissed her, he ran his free hand over her ass cheeks, molding them to his form. Worse, he even had the audacity to finger the tiny fabric of her thong that rested between her cheeks. She felt exposed to the wild night when he hiked her knee-length skirt up to her waist. Tyrana wasn't sure what thrilled her more. His fingers probing her body in places she never dared imagine from a man or the feel of the cool night air on her naked flesh. Both stimulated her so much she groaned into his mouth.

"Rough it is," he said, promptly hoisting her onto his shoulders like she was a child. Then he proceeded to march with her through the forest. With her head bobbing down his chiseled back, she had the best view in the world—his glorious ass. Mesmerized, she watched as the muscles in each cheek vibrated when he walked.

"Once we're free of this blasted forest, I plan to make you ache with pleasure. So, my little filly, look all you want at my ass, because by the time morning comes, yours is going to be mine."

Ohh, how dare he. She fought the grin of sweet anticipation that came over her face. Tyrana vowed that once she was free of him, she planned to show him just who was master when it came to the art of sex play.

Rusty halted. Every hair on his body stood on end. The trees were trying to surround them. "Blast the forest guardians," he muttered to himself.

The moon was bright and full, its light casting a path through the forest that told him they weren't going to make it. If he had been smart, he wouldn't have dallied with the sexy Maida woman called Mira. She was the cause of all of this.

Rusty couldn't flash into anything, let alone his true self, a Mage Pegcentaur, because then...well he'd have to keep her, or worse, kill her. He snorted. Keeping her was out of the question and the thought of killing the sexy hellcat caused his heart to skip a beat.

He did, though, plan on keeping her long enough to enjoy every piece of her lush body. After that he'd take her back to her lands. That would mean a third trip through the Dark Forest and into enemy territory. *Ugh!* What had started out as a simple errand for his friend was now anything but.

"Put me down, now!" bellowed the domineering woman.

Hell's bells, she never lets up, does she? Even when he had told her countless times to keep her mouth shut, she liked to get the last word in. When he thought about her mouth or her lips, his cock bucked to attention. What she had done—taking the full length of his long, thick cock deep within her tight, wet mouth, caused his stones to ache with a heaviness he'd not felt since his *youngling* days as a mere Pegcentaur.

Rusty knew he'd been shocked. If his friend could have seen him, Tulon would have laughed his ass off. For two years Tulon had been held as a prisoner by the Maida. The stories he had told Rusty hadn't shocked him as much as Mira's actions.

He had thought he'd tasted every type of *rutting* possible after his many visits to Mount Atrophe, the pleasure place for his kind, but apparently not. Once he had them safely through the forest, he planned on letting the sexy little filly have her fill of him.

Placing her gently on the forest floor, he motioned for her to be quiet. Thankfully, she had enough common sense to heed his warning.

"What's wrong with the trees?" she asked, her voice barely a whisper.

Hushing her with his finger, he squatted, placing both hands palms down on the forest floor. Clearing his mind, he tried yet again to communicate with one of the forest guardians.

The woman squatted next to him. "What are you doing?" she asked, clearly perplexed by his actions.

Like he was about to disclose his intentions. "If you could be quiet and let me concentrate, then maybe I can get us out of here in one piece." He cleared his mind again, trying hard to ignore her flowery scent, even as he realized she smelled like wild lilies. He stifled a groan when he realized even her scent was distracting him. Shuffling a foot away from her, he placed his hands again on the ground and fought to focus.

"That I'd love to see. So tell me, how does one get out of a forest simply by praying?" she snapped, standing up to move away from him.

Praying? The woman thinks I'm praying. Well, maybe. Usually though his prayers went unanswered. Out of the corner of his eye, Rusty caught the tree's movement. Grabbing her by the arm, he pushed her back. The tree, none too happy to have its prize removed from its grasp, tore up its roots and shuffled toward where the woman lay.

He could tell by her wide-eyed look that she was shocked. *Well, she'd best get that little ass of hers in high gear, now!* He positioned himself between the towering angry tree and the Maida woman.

"Move it, now!" he commanded, yanking on her arm to propel her to her feet and forward in one fluid motion.

"Where do I go? And what, by the Saints, is that?" she screeched.

Her fear lanced his heart. He was using as much magic as possible to keep the forest at bay, but his powers weren't fully recharged. Stopping the poison from the eye-asp snake had already drained him. He needed a full day before his magic would be at its height again. But the time for talk was later. Now they simply had to get out of the forest guardians' territory or risk becoming a crunchy midnight snack.

"Go straight. Keep running...no matter what. I'll be right behind you. Now move it." He forced his voice to be authoritative yet calm.

"I can't just leave you," she said, darting her head left and right as more trees slowly awoke from their slumber.

"You won't be leaving me and I can take care of myself. You can't. Move it. Now!" Rusty pushed her toward the barely discernable path. He watched as she hesitated one second and then darted through the trees. When he judged her to be a safe distance away, he let his magic loose and transformed into a Mage Pegcentaur. His legs were shaky from the quick flash but he willed himself to stand. Then his wings easily lifted him off the forest ground and he took flight.

Once he cleared the top canopy of the trees, he watched as the Maida woman scrambled through the forest. He longed to help her but knew he couldn't. In another few wingbeats she'd be safe. Then Rusty viewed the crest of a cliff and the long plunge to the river below. He realized in a heartbeat what he should have known all along. The woman had no way down the cliff, unless she dove straight into the turbulent water below. He highly doubted she would do that. He had always flashed himself deep into the Dark Forest. He cursed himself for not securing a safe way out for the Maida woman.

While trying to figure a way to help her, he watched her clear the forest, never once breaking stride. Her athletic stamina was a bonus. In a blink, she crested the cliff and placed her hands high above her head.

She wouldn't dare, he thought, watching in total disbelief as she dove head-first into the dark pool of water below. Rusty's heart lurched to his feet. For one dreadful minute, he felt the shift of magic as his form shimmered with uncertainty and dread.

Chapter Five

Piercing cold, dark murky water swallowed her body whole, submerging her limbs in a black abyss, paralyzing her to a tedium of slow-motion movements. One arm inched forward, up over her head to grasp a long stalk of water grass—an anchor of sorts to the surface above. A second hand grabbed another stem, enabling Tyrana to propel herself upward.

Her heart beat rapidly in her chest and her lungs burned, almost ripping her apart with the urge to take a breath. But a breath meant death. She would not succumb willingly to the dark water. Tyrana kicked, forcing the numbing cold to a corner of her mind, willing her legs to move. Movement brought pain, and a thousand needles felt as if they were drilling into her calves. She fought to ignore it.

An air bubble cascaded up toward the surface. Tyrana blinked hard, attempting to follow the bubble up. She kicked hard again, laboring to move her arms up. Then light from above beamed at her. The surface gleamed freedom and life, giving her the strength to push beyond her limit. After what seemed like an eternity, her head finally crested the churning water. She greedily gulped breaths of oxygen and eyed the shoreline, which seemed far away.

But Tyrana didn't survive the current that had attempted to yank her down to the river's bottom without a fight just to fail because the safety of land seemed impossibly out of reach. No. With determination setting her strokes she angled her body up and out of the water, concentrating on putting one arm in front of the other.

Only when her feet skimmed a large boulder did she feel reassured she'd actually make it. Exhausted, yet rejuvenated at the same time, she crawled on hands and knees to get out of the frigid water.

"What, by all the Saints, were you thinking? You could have been killed," said Rusty, standing two feet in front of her, completely dry and looking as pissed off as you please.

How by the Saints did he get here without getting soaked from the river? wondered Tyrana. Without acknowledging him, she stood and strode past him. Soaked to the bone, she unfastened the straps to her leather halter top and whipped it over her head. By the man's indrawn breath, she knew she had his attention. Feeling very much like a naughty hellcat, she was ticked off to the core at his commanding attitude and she was mightily peeved he had somehow escaped the forest without getting wet. The breeze from the night air felt strangely warm on her cool skin.

And thank you so much for all your help. Baby, it's payback time. So, you think you can master me. Think again. By the time I am through with you...you will be begging me.

Turning her head to give him a shy look, she unclasped her belt buckle, letting it fall to the sandy beach. Then she shimmied out of her soaked knee-length skirt and leaned over to drape it over a large boulder, knowing her provocative pose would provide him with a good view of her ass. Then she turned and faced him boldly.

Licking her lips, she notched up her chin, all but daring him. "For your information, I was saving my ass."

Then she hooked two fingers in her black thong and shamelessly lowered it down over her cold cheeks and legs. Once she was free of it, she stood, slightly embarrassed but letting him look his fill. It was a highly titillating moment for her. He was still clothed in his tight brown breeches and she was as naked as the day she was born.

She knew her actions were spurring him on. His cock bulged between his legs. Tyrana could have sworn she heard him growl but she wasn't done with him yet. By the time she let him anywhere near her body, he'd be all but ready to explode.

Turning so that her backside was his only view, she strode forward to a large flat boulder. Then she sat down facing him, her legs slightly spread. She watched as his eyes darkened to deep shade of emerald and his nostrils flared. Then wickedly she stroked her body from her neck to her breasts, down to her legs with her own two hands. She let her hands travel several times over her body and then casually moved them to cup her breasts, which were already peaked from the cool night air.

"By the blessed Saints, I'm in heaven," he moaned, as he rubbed his thick bulge through his breeches. Then she watched as he moved forward.

That wouldn't do at all. "Not so fast. You can watch but there's no sampling tonight," she said, sitting up slightly on the large boulder.

Tyrana knew if he moved any closer, she'd lose the game. She wanted him so bad she felt her cream slide down onto her inner thighs. Even greater than her need for him was the desire to make him suffer.

"Look, my little filly, let me get this straight. You plan on taking your own pleasure and I get to watch?"

Tyrana nodded.

"Hell's bells, keep at it," he replied, once again reaching into his tight breeches to free his long shaft.

Tyrana knew she groaned. His cock was thick and it glistened with his own cream. She burned to have it plunge deep inside of her. But if he took his pleasure while she did, that wouldn't do either.

"Put it back," she said, stopping her hands from roaming over her sensitive body.

He choked on a cough. "Put it back. So you get to pleasure yourself and I get to ache. That's your game plan, isn't it? My, aren't we a hellcat who likes to play with her prey."

A teasing grin lit his face. She found it oddly endearing. She stifled the moan that was on the tip of her tongue as she watched him stroke his thick member twice more and then with a wink, he plunged it back into his breeches.

"Just remember my promise to you earlier, because I never go back on a promise," he said, bracing his legs in a wide stance.

Tyrana gulped. The man looked warrior ready to pounce on her. How could she forget his promise? Without a doubt, this man set her pulse racing. She forced her heart to slow down. Tyrana was determined to go through with her plan.

Once she determined he would stay in place, she cleared her mind and set about teasing herself. She pinched her nipples, watching as they hardened more. She pulled at them harder than any man dared, twisting and tweaking them, loving the feel of pain and pleasure as it spiraled through her body. She raised her legs onto the boulder so her feet were flat and her knees were slightly parted. Then she opened them so her wet pussy glistened at him in the moonlight.

She heard his mumbling as he fought for control. She gave him a sly look. His body was rigid and a tick had begun at his jaw. He clenched and unclenched his fists at his side. And she loved it. There was also a small wet stain where the tip of his shaft touched his tight breeches. She knew without a doubt he was experiencing as much sexual frustration as she had earlier and that fueled her desire.

Slowly, she moved her hand over her flat tummy to the crest of curls covering her sex. Then she opened her legs wider and fingered her slick folds.

"You like?" she asked saucily, as she darted a finger into her cunt.

"By the Saints, you are going to pay big time," he muttered. "Taste it," he demanded.

Even though a part of her resented his commanding tone, she did as instructed. A hearty groan from him was her reward.

Eyeing him, she asked, "What else should I do?"

"Take that finger of yours and plunge it deep inside your pussy," he demanded, his words a growl as he gritted his teeth.

"Just one finger?" she replied, doing as instructed.

"Hell's bells...my little filly. You know I'm in agony," he replied, moving his hand to rub his bulge.

"No touching," she replied. She watched as he forced his hand to return to his side. The tick at his jaw throbbed double time.

"Two fingers and pinch your nipples harder," he demanded.

His eyes glazed over with desire as she did as instructed.

"Now with your other hand, tap your nub."

"Like this," replied Tyrana, moaning from the sweet sensation of her nub pebbling to attention as she splayed her legs open even more.

"Now turn over."

"What?"

"You heard me, turn over. I want to watch your ass move as you pleasure yourself," he said, his fists clenching and unclenching all the while.

She had forgotten how much he had liked her ass. So be it. She turned over on the large rock so that she was on her knees, her bottom high and exposed. She said a silent thanks that she had picked a large smooth flat boulder as she let her body weight adjust to being held by her knees.

"Will this do?" She turned and winked at him as she jiggled her ass.

In a blink, he was behind her. Before she could demand he move away, she felt his hands on her ass. Heat flared deep within her core shooting straight to her womb. She couldn't have spoken if she tried. A whimper of need escaped her.

"Put your knees together more," he replied, the entire time stroking her ass.

Complying, her body waited. What was he going to do to her now? The uncertainty of what he had in mind aroused her more than if he'd placed his hands on her. She had never been commanded by a man before. Both his tone and that blasted voice of his sizzled all her nerve endings. Her body all but screamed for him to touch her.

"This has got to be the best blasted ass I've ever seen and I plan on making it mine."

Before she could question what he meant, she felt the gentle scrape of his teeth as he nipped first one cheek and then the other. The gesture was oddly sensual, erotic and sensitive.

Then he kissed her cheeks while roaming his hands over her ass. When he slid a finger down her crack, her body stilled. He moved his hand lower and slid a finger through her wet folds and then back up to the crack of her ass. She shivered. He repeated that over and over again, causing her to squirm with a need she couldn't describe.

One of his hands snaked up to her front. He went straight to her peaked nipples and tweaked them hard, causing her to moan and shuffle back on her knees. She felt the tip of his wet cock on her ass. For one moment she wondered when he had removed his breeches, but then he slid his shaft between her cheeks moving it down to her wet pussy. All rational thoughts fled as her body tingled in sweet anticipation of the feel of him.

"Mine," he muttered, lowering his body to cover hers. His lips trailed hot kisses up her back where he nibbled on her neck. She arched her neck, letting him suckle her skin, enjoying the bruise she knew it would leave. She felt the bite of his teeth at the same time she felt his thick member probing at her ass.

What's he doing? She shuffled back, trying to reposition his member so it could slide into her wet opening.

"I told you that ass was going to be mine, so relax," he said, once again positioning his body over hers. This time she felt his finger at her ass, and before she could say anything, he plunged it into her slick, tight opening. The sensation of it, the erotic violation of her body caused her to groan. Then he pumped it, while one hand moved from one nipple to the other to tweak them into submission.

"Well, well, well, nothing like a virgin ass to make mine," he said, his voice working its magic into her being so that she relaxed into his hold.

When the hand that had been tweaking her nipples moved to her nub, she squirmed back, hating that she loved the feel of his finger up her ass while he pleasured her. He was a blasted expert. He took her nub between two fingers until it throbbed with need. She was so close to climaxing she couldn't help but squirm and moan with a fiery need.

"Not yet, my little filly," he said.

"Put that cock of yours in me!" she demanded, arching into him, needing the feel of his fullness deep inside of her.

"Where?" he drawled on the word, as he sucked on her neck.

She knew he wanted her to say it, just like she had ached for his erotic words while she had pleasured herself. *Fine. Anything to get that thick shaft inside of me before I scream every foul word I can think of.* The need was so intense Tyrana thought she'd black out from it soon.

"In my ass." She moaned the words as she squirmed against the wet tip of his cock.

"Ahh, that's what I thought."

Then she felt it. His cock was slick from their combined juices. She felt him open her ass cheeks and then gently push at her opening. It felt so blasted good. She was so tight, he was so thick, that the sensation of complete fullness soon took over all her senses. She knew he was taking his time as, inch by thick inch, he pushed his cock into her tight opening. She wanted more. Pushing hard against him, she was rewarded when the fullness of him lodged deep within her.

She heard him mumble, "By the blessed Saints."

Thankfully he started to move. And for the first time in her life, Tyrana gave herself up completely to a man. She let him take her like a beast. It was a highly liberating feeling. He plunged mercilessly over and over into her ass, his thick, long cock stretching her completely. He grabbed her front and positioned her so she was even higher on her knees as he rocked her back and forth. One hand played with her nub until she ached from the intensity of it.

Then when he knew she could no longer stand it, he opened her swollen folds and plunged a finger into her wet opening. She felt full with him. He claimed all of her. He was in her ass pounding into her while two of his fingers pumped over and over again into her wet pussy. She climaxed so hard she screamed.

He groaned, the sound a deep vibrating rumble. When he spilled his seed into her, she felt a second wave of climax claim her.

Never in her life had she ever been pleasured so brutally...yet so lovingly. She knew she should feel ashamed at letting a man take complete control of her but she didn't. She felt complete like never before and that terrified her.

Chapter Six

Rusty chuckled to himself as he spooned his body tight to the Maida woman. She was asleep to the world, which was a good thing. The little filly had indeed surprised him. Now, thanks to her sizzling passion, he was at his peak, so to speak. He grimaced as his shaft once again bucked to life against her luscious body.

Still in la-la land, the woman had no idea that in a blink, with his magic back to full power, he had transported them back to the Plains. *Home never looked so sweet.* He relished the scent of the lush green meadow mixed with wildflowers and the light dusty feel of the morning sun breaking through the horizon. If he was in his Mage Pegcentaur form, he would have unfurled his massive wings to soar through the dawn sky.

He had always loved the feel of the sun's rays on his sensitive flight feathers. The possibilities always seemed endless with the breaking of each new day. Maybe that was the creature within him. He wondered idly, as a finger traced the Maida woman's breast, why he felt compelled to bring her to the Plains and not flash her back to Maida territory.

He felt the woman called Mira arch into his body. Instantly his cock jumped and thickened even more as all his blood pooled to that one sensitive region of his body. He stifled the groan even as he caught the scent of her—all woman, combined with sex and a hint of wild lilies. The mix was intoxicating as it cascaded through his system.

He lifted his head to watch her face as she fought to wake up. Her eyelashes were long and dark. He liked how her eyebrows were a lighter shade of brown than her hair and how they neatly arched. *Perky eyebrows on an otherwise serious face.* She had a dusting of freckles dotting her nose and both cheeks. By far her best facial feature was her red, full sensual lips. They begged a man to throw caution to the wind, to reach out and kiss them, to suck on them, nip them and mold them to his own. By the Saints, how he wanted to once again sample her lips. This time he couldn't help the guttural groan that escaped him.

In an instant, she went from sleep to complete alertness. In one heartbeat, her baby blue eyes, which mirrored a cloudless sky, calculated everything that had happened. She blinked once and then pushed him away.

Rusty regretted in that moment that he had clothed them when he had flashed them to the Plains. He was back in his form-fitting breeches—*blasted things humans wore to cover their own nudity.* He had clad her once again in her knee-length skirt and leather halter top. How he wished he had overlooked clothing her in that top. What he wouldn't give for a peek of her lush, ivory-colored breasts and those dusty-rose colored nipples of hers he had pebbled and suckled on until he had almost spilled his seed like a *youngling.*

"Where are we?" Her voice was still husky with sleep.

He watched as she sat and took in her environment. Her eyes widened and he sensed her fear. He could just imagine what she thought. How by the Mother Earth was he going to explain this to the Maida woman? On the Plains below them was his clan. Other Mage Pegcentaurs grazing on the dew-covered grass, some were even beginning their morning archery drills. No one had spotted them yet, thanks to his shield.

Then he realized the woman was laughing. "Ooh, this is good, very good. Wake me up when it's over, will you," she said, yawning.

Then she promptly lay back down on the grass and turned her back to him. *She thinks she's dreaming.* The realization hit him like a downpour. He didn't like it one bit.

"We're at the Plains," he said, a hint of anger evident in his voice.

"Yeah, right. How did we get here?" she asked, still not bothering to turn over.

"I flashed us here."

"Uh huh, that makes sense."

The woman was making him mad. His kind never lied. Didn't she know he was telling the truth? He'd have to spell it out for her. He didn't like that idea one bit. *Maybe I should talk to the Mage Council first before letting another Maida woman learn about the inherent magic that makes up Mother Earth.*

Rusty didn't like his options. He sent a silent command to every member on the Plains to flash into human form and to cover themselves with clothing. He knew without question they would obey. He would explain everything to them later, after he'd sorted out what to say to the Maida woman.

Drugs. That blasted man must have slipped me something. Tyrana was so mad she wouldn't have been surprised to see smoke come out of her ears. *Or could it have been a reaction to the best sex I've ever had in my life?* That ridiculous notion eased the swell of anger she felt.

Tyrana had no idea where she was. Someplace he called the Plains. *Like that's a landmark I'd recognize.* Obviously he had somehow brought her there, which shocked her. But how?

Propping herself up on her elbows, she watched the man stand to his towering height. He took her breath away. He didn't look like any Maida man she'd known. Or act like one either, Tyrana thought.

Her heart thundered with dread. Could he be a renegade Maida warrior? She had heard rumors some Maida men had escaped and were forming small warrior bands in their feeble attempt to overthrow the current government. She had thought they were just that—rumors. Now she wasn't so sure.

She watched him move away from her. Her eyes were immediately drawn to his ass and the long, muscular length of his legs. He practically galloped as he made his way down the hill. Then it dawned on her that he was leaving her.

She stood, placed both hands on her hips and said, "Just where do you think you're going?"

He didn't break stride once or acknowledge her question. Halfway down the hill, she realized he had dismissed her. The shock of that angered her.

She marched after him, fully intending for him to explain himself to her once and for all. She had to stop herself from running after him. That wouldn't do her any good. She had to remind herself to act dignified. Once she was close enough, she'd kick him where it counted.

Cresting the second hill, the sight that greeted her stilled her racing heart. Over one hundred men gleamed in the morning sun as they went through some sort of warrior drill. Each was armed with a strange looking weapon that reminded her of an old-fashioned dueling lance. The lances were twice her height and each had a metallic shiny arrowhead at the tip. They looked deadly.

She was spellbound as each man performed some strange sort of warrior dance in slow motion. First they'd spin the dueling lances above their heads, then, in a wide sweep, they went under their feet as they jumped high in the air. The lance was then used to perform quick jabs in front of them and then they'd be squatting, kicking one leg high in the air while balancing the lance with one arm. And then they'd begin the slow-moving dance again.

"It's beautiful," she said, breathlessly, not realizing she'd spoken until Rusty's husky voice seared her core.

"Ahh, that it is. It's called the *kel'am'tar*. It takes years of practice," he said, with obvious pride.

His words slowly penetrated her dazed mind. "You can do that?"

He turned to look at her over his shoulder. She felt his dark green eyes appraise her. "Ahh, I can do that and a lot more."

Tyrana took a good look around at her strange surroundings. Nothing looked remotely similar to Maida. There were no manicured lawns lining neat pathways. There was no four-story central building. In fact, there weren't any buildings at all. At the bottom of the hill there was a cluster of small round thatched huts but they certainly weren't large enough to hold an extended family.

And just where are all the women? All I see are men. Not that she was minding the men but it only confirmed her worst fear.

"So, you are a rogue warrior." She crossed her arms over her chest and stared at him.

"I am a warrior, yes, but not a rogue. Welcome to the Plains, my Maida lady. Come and meet a few of my fellow warrior friends."

A large welcoming smile lit up his face, melting Tyrana's anger like a douse of water. She realized meeting the other rogue men was her chance to gather intelligence for the Maida warrior-women.

Did he just call me my Maida lady? Her breasts tingled both from his voice and the sweet endearment of his choice of words. She watched as he held out his hand to her in another old-fashioned gesture. Strangely, she was touched deeply by his actions.

She took his offered hand, telling herself it meant nothing. The feel of his large warm hand tingled her skin into awareness of him.

"Hilt, I'd like you to meet Mira," said Rusty, beckoning a dark-haired man forward.

The man was breathtakingly beautiful. A quick look around and Tyrana realized all the men were extremely handsome. They were all physically fit and all ruggedly masculine, each in their own way.

So this is why I can't find a feisty man. They have all become rogue warriors. Go figure.

Hilt bowed low, crossing his arm over his waist. Again, the old-fashioned gesture disarmed her. She smiled.

"Another Maida treasure, I see," said Hilt.

Tyrana wasn't sure what he meant about that comment, but she liked the hot, sexy appraisal Hilt gave her body.

She decided to up her sexy charms. "The pleasure is all mine," she said, lowering her voice. She watched as the dark irises of his pupils dilated in sexual awareness.

"Well, if the pleasure is all yours, whatever shall I do to please you?" Hilt's voice too lowered and rumbled like Rusty's, straight through her system.

"You had best finish practicing the *kel'am'tar,* Hilt, before I pleasure you with pain," said Rusty.

The harsh, commanding tone in his voice broke Tyrana's happy mood. *Grumpy, grumpy, beastly man.*

"Why don't we show your Maida lady friend the *kel'am'tar* in the ancient way," said Hilt.

"Are you challenging me?" asked Rusty.

"For the right of pleasuring this beautiful Maida lady. I do believe I am," said Hilt, backing up to bow again formally, first to her and then to Rusty.

It was then Tyrana noticed that the men were no longer performing their morning warrior-dance. In fact, every eye seemed to be riveted on the three of them. *Now this isn't good. Not good at all.*

"Okay, men, that's enough. As flattered as I am, you can go back to your little warrior games," said Tyrana, turning to walk away from the men.

Rusty's hold on her arm stilled her actions. "Let me go," she snapped.

"I don't think so," he said, with a cool, calculating look in his eyes. "You will stand here and watch. And do your part."

Tyrana tried to twist her arm out of his hold. It was no use. "Look, he's kidding, right?"

Rusty shook his head. "Hilt, you understand what your actions mean?"

"It means that I will soon get to plunge my cock into that sweet, wet opening that is ripe for the picking," answered Hilt.

Tyrana knew his words were meant to shock her, but they didn't. Somehow, she felt as if his words were meant more to provoke Rusty. *Why would that be?*

"She's mine," said Rusty.

He let go of her but she stood rooted to the spot. Tyrana knew full well making a run for it would do her no good—he'd bring her right back. She blinked as both men stripped off their clothing. Two magnificently beautiful men stood before her. Her core muscles clenched hard with need.

"Like what you see?" taunted Hilt, holding his impressive member in his hand.

"She might but if that's your weapon of choice, I'm afraid it's not very impressive," snapped Rusty, holding his own engorged cock with one hand as he pumped it fast for show, while with casual grace he caught the long double-edge lance that was thrown his way with one hand

I know I'm dreaming. This is one of my weird, barbaric erotic dreams. She couldn't seem to pry her eyes away from the men. Each seemed intent on displaying their sexual prowess to her while they prepared to fight each other. *Maybe pinching myself will wake me up.*

Tyrana wasn't entirely sure she wanted to awaken as the men calmly circled each other. Each one held onto their rock hard members while wielding the double-edged lance.

"Now remove your clothing, Mira," commanded Rusty.

"What?" she squeaked, her dream-like thoughts evaporating.

"Take off your clothes," replied Hilt.

"Okay, look you two. If you want to play your barbaric he-man ritual with each other, go straight ahead. But as much as I'm enjoying the scene of the two of you playing with yourselves, I most certainly am not going to remove one stitch of clothing for your amusement." She crossed her arms over her chest to stress her point.

"Remove them, Mira. Now!" shouted Rusty.

Tyrana watched as he stood in a warrior stance, eyeing his opponent.

"Go to Hell," she snapped and turned her back on the men.

"Shall I do it for you?" taunted Hilt.

"I will," replied Rusty. "She's not used to our ways. I will explain it to her."

"You can explain all you want, Rusty, but I will not take off my clothes," she said, keeping her back to the two men.

She felt the warmth of Rusty before his two hands took her by the shoulders and turned her toward him.

"The *kel'am'tar* is an ancient warrior challenge that was designed by the wise women. To stop the duels to the death, they, as wise women, came up with another more sensitive, yet highly skilled challenge. Whoever spills their seed first and sheds first blood gets banished. The last warrior still standing claims leadership and you as the prize. Your job is to sexually distract us enough so that one of us spills our seed. Are you up the challenge, Mira? The power is in your hands."

Rusty's eyes gleamed at her, keenly. She shook her head to focus—hating how the sound of his voice swamped her with need.

The power is in my hands? "Let me get this straight. I'm supposed to perform some strip act for the two of you while you each try to draw blood with those weapons and you think I'm calling the shots." Sarcasm laced her words.

"You are calling the shots. And I don't intend to lose. Afraid?"

"Me, afraid...you are kidding? I'm not the one with the double-edged lance."

"I think you're afraid. And here I thought Maida women weren't afraid of anything...seems like I'm wrong."

That's it. Tyrana simmered. She knew he was trying to rile her, and worse, it was working. "You think you're man enough to not spill your seed. Want to bet?" She flashed a slow seductive smile at him.

Chapter Seven

"Good, then let's get on with it," said Rusty, stroking his shaft, letting her eyes get a good, long heated look at his thick cock.

"Fine, let's begin," she said, fingering a clasp on her leather halter top.

"Took you long enough," said Hilt, cupping his stones to get Mira's attention.

"You two can begin. I'm going to do this my way," said Tyrana, unclasping one button on her top. Slowly, she let her hands circle her breasts as they strained against the leather. She moaned throatily, letting them hear her desire.

By the Saints, how I love that sound. Rusty forced himself to concentrate on the task at hand.

"Are her breasts as milky white as I think they are?" asked Hilt, trying to disarm Rusty with his words and actions.

"Aye, they are. And her nipples are the color of rosebuds and they taste sweet," taunted Rusty, knowing his words were working as Hilt swallowed hard.

They both heard the rustle of material as Mira dropped her leather top to the ground. Both eyes were drawn for a quick glance.

"By the blessed Mother, they are a delight," drawled Hilt, taking a step forward to plunge the *avikel,* the double-edged lance, straight at Rusty.

"I'd love the feel of a man's fingers right now pebbling my nipples," said Mira, tweaking her nipples with her own fingers.

Rusty's eyes were drawn to the sight of what she was doing even as his warrior training kicked in and he sidestepped Hilt's hit.

It was hard work, watching Mira pleasure her delicious body and being aware of Hilt. But he was aware enough to see Hilt lick his lips, eyeing Mira as she slowly shimmied out of her skirt. Rusty jabbed to the left of Hilt, hoping to mark him even as his cock bulged more.

Rusty couldn't help but pump it unconsciously as the scent of Mira, hot and ready, soared through his senses.

Hilt turned at the last moment so that his body was an inch closer to Mira.

Rusty could barely move as Mira bent over provocatively with her ass gleaming in the morning sun. She then cast a shy glance over her shoulder at both of them and proceeded to lick her finger in a slow, provocative move that resonated straight to his shaft. Rusty held his breath. He heard Hilt's indrawn groan.

Together, as each man circled the other, they cast glances her way. Each watched as she continued to slowly lick her finger and then run it up and down her body, over her breasts, teasing her peaked nipples to her open, splayed legs as she bent at the knees. *That submissive pose is my favorite.*

"Is she a good ride?" asked Hilt.

Rusty knew the question was meant to help Hilt focus—not that he intended to help.

He strode forward, circling the long *avikel* high over his head with one hand as he pumped his cock, giving into the wild need to prance before his lady. "She likes it rough. Her cream tastes like warm honey and when I'm done with you, Hilt, Mira will be too sore to walk for days."

"What is she doing?" asked Hilt, watching as Mira got up from her knees to saunter over toward another Mage Pegcentaur.

"I'm not sure," answered Rusty, loving how her large breasts bobbed and swayed as she walked.

Both men took the opportunity to lunge repeatedly at each other.

"Ahh, now this is much better."

Rusty heard Mira's moan and couldn't stop himself from looking. It was a sight that made all the hairs on his body tingle.

Mira had positioned her body flat with her back on the ground. Her legs were splayed in a v-shape, wide open and her glistening cunt was openly on display. She held a long, thick stick that looked as if she'd wrapped it in soft leather and greased it. Then she plunged it into her pussy. The act shocked him.

"By all that's holy...she's incredible," groaned Hilt as he stroked his shaft hard.

Rusty knew exactly how he felt. Sweat broke out on his forehead as he balanced the *avikel* with one hand while pumping his cock more with the other. The tip was wet. He tried to think of some stupid thing to refocus his concentration on the task at hand. However the sight of Mira, who had now repositioned herself with her legs in the air so both men could see her plunge the homemade dildo inside her channel, had him gritting his teeth.

Her throaty moans and groans told him she was on the edge of climaxing.

"She's going to come. I can't believe your luck," said Hilt.

Rusty watched as his friend fell to his knees with a loud groan while Mira pumped the makeshift dildo into her pussy with a fierce need and came. Rusty didn't hesitate. His *avikel* sliced across Hilt's chest as the younger Mage Pegcentaur spilled his seed.

Rusty didn't think his friend even felt the painful slice. His eyes were glazed with passion as his seed fell to the ground.

Dropping the *avikel*, Rusty marched over to where Mira lay with her legs wide open. Without preamble, he removed the homemade dildo from her pussy and plunged his own engorged cock deep inside of her. *To hell with finesse.*

Somewhere at the base of his consciousness, he remembered they were both on display but that too didn't matter. In the heat of the moment, he needed to claim his prize, his woman.

He pounded into her. "You are mine. Every inch of you is mine. I claim you." Rusty roared the words loudly, letting everyone know he marked her as his. He forced her legs up over his shoulders, slipped his hands under her ass and plunged deeply into her. He filled her, touched her womb and came, letting the magic of his seed seep into her.

Consequences be damned. He felt her clutch his ass, clawing his shoulders as she tried to climb onto his lap, reaching for that pinnacle of pleasure. As he pressed a finger into her ass, her inner muscles clenched his cock tightly and she came. He bit her roughly on the shoulder, knowing it was too late to stop his actions.

Instinct had taken hold of him. He gave and gave, letting a part of the magic that was within him flow through her system. He felt a moment of hesitation when she realized something strange was happening to her. Again he plunged deep, his shaft thickening more, not wanting to give her the chance to think about it.

He leaned down and kissed her, branding her lips as his. Then he reached between them, found her nub and pebbled it until she peaked. When she came the third time, he lifted her up onto his lap and pumped his seed into her again. Her legs fell from his shoulders to hug his hips. She was limp from sex.

"Now that's what I call a champion's welcome," he said.

Chapter Eight

"Sorry about that. Couldn't help myself," he said, grinning like a well-satisfied domestic cat. Tyrana knew there was nothing domestic about this man.

She wasn't sure who had actually won that bizarre warrior duel but she certainly felt as if she had. *Sweet Mother, if my body feels this good simply from him banging into me ferociously, how would it feel if we actually took the time to leisurely explore every inch of each other or, better yet, take the time to experiment.*

She licked her lips, loving that delicious thought.

He pulled her to her feet, found her clothing and then helped her dress. She found his actions oddly charming and endearing. By this time, most of the men had either resumed their training or had gone on to other tasks. She noticed Hilt was nowhere to be seen.

"You like winning," she said, buckling her halter top up.

Still wearing nothing, he placed both hands on his hips. "Only if you're the prize."

Then Tyrana heard a familiar sound dredging up that old ache she thought she had banished.

She watched Rusty turn to grab his discarded clothing. He dressed quickly. "What is she doing?" he mumbled to himself as he buttoned his breeches.

Tyrana assumed he was referring to none other than her sister, who was attempting to run straight toward them. Tyrana felt heat bloom all over her skin. Her sister, Rowena, looked extremely pregnant. Envy and a cold yearning slammed hard into her. She forced herself to look away. Tyrana turned her back to her sister, hoping Rowena would get the hint.

"Ohh, by the Saints, I can't believe you did it. You did it, Rusty. You did it!" shouted Rowena, continuing to huff her way up to where they stood.

Tyrana moved even further away from Rusty. She longed to run straight back into the Dark Forest. Instead she fought her own inner battle and forced herself to stop moving.

Rowena ran straight past Rusty to where she stood. Great, this is great. *Why is she here? And does she have to wear that awful dress that shows every round curve of her belly?* Tyrana knew she was jealous. *Bitch that I am, so what?*

"Thank you so much, Rusty," said Rowena. "Ty, I'm so glad you came. I just knew that you would. This is perfect. Absolutely perfect," said Rowena, still slightly out of breath from her jaunt.

Tyrana didn't say anything. She stood rigidly still. *Please don't hug me.* Tyrana was afraid she'd give into the tears that threatened to fall if her sister actually touched her.

"What are you talking about, Rowena? This isn't your sister. This is Mira," said Rusty, looking at Rowena in disbelief.

"That's funny, Rusty. Don't be an idiot. This is my sister. This is Tyrana," said Rowena, ignoring Tyrana's silent plea not to touch her.

Tyrana stood her ground, allowing her sister to embrace her. It was an awkward moment for them both.

"I knew you'd come. You've made me so happy, Ty. Wait until you meet Tulon. You're going to love him."

"So, Sis, how far along are you?" asked Tyrana, choking back a sob. She prayed no one heard the tightness in her voice.

"Sis! What are you talking about, Mira?" shouted Rusty, looking less and less pleased as the seconds ticked by and he realized he had been duped.

She noticed that tick had started in his jaw again. *Not good...not good at all.*

"Oops, I might have misled you a bit," stated Tyrana.

"A bit!" His voice roared over the lush meadow, causing more than a few heads to turn their way.

"Don't get all hot-headed on me. My name is Mira. Actually it's Tyrana Mira Susan Dana Faydon to be precise. I did tell you a name," she said, shrugging her shoulders, not liking his disparaging tone of voice.

"You lied to me. That's just great. Guess you got what you wanted, Rowena. I can't believe this." Rusty mumbled his words as he walked away from the two of them.

Tyrana tried to shake free from Rowena. Her sister wasn't normally into tender embraces and she was slightly ashamed at how good it felt.

"I'm not sure what kind of trouble you caused but I don't care. I can't believe you came," said Rowena, her sky-blue eyes brimming with tears.

"I didn't come for you. I came for him," muttered Tyrana, forcibly moving out of her sister's arms. She took two steps back to provide much needed space between them.

"Him! Oh, you don't even know him."

Tyrana grinned devilishly. "I know all I need to."

Her sister sighed and there was a cautious glint in her eyes, which Tyrana found disconcerting.

"I highly doubt you know all about him. You'll never change," admonished her sister.

Tyrana crossed her arms over her chest. "That's right, Sis. I'll never change...get that through your thick head. It's all fun and games for me."

"No it's not, Ty. That's not the real you talking."

Tyrana took a step closer to her sister, invading her precious personal space she always prided herself on. "Actually, Roe, that is the real me talking, you just never listen...you always hear what you want to hear."

The next thing she'd get was a lecture on how to behave properly, how to be a "good" sister. Well, Rowena could take all that "good" and shove it up her ass. Tyrana hated how annoyed she felt at her little sister's big-sister act. *When did I let that happen? And why do I even care? She'll never understand the real me and I certainly don't want to disappoint.*

Tyrana strolled past her sister. She knew she had some fast talking to do to bridge the gap that now existed between her and Rusty and that weighed more on her soul than listening to another lecture from her sister. But more importantly, she had to get home. She forced herself not to recall the memory of her sister's bulging belly as it bumped her stomach. She had barely recovered from the shock of finding out her sister was the fertile one, but now this...it was too much to bear. The longing of what she could never have caused her womb to clench. Tyrana fought hard to control the crest of tears that washed her eyes. She shook her head, clearing her mind, determined to get control of her emotions. *No sense crying over something that can never be.*

Chapter Nine

Rusty couldn't believe his luck. *Sis! As in sister!* He snorted. *Of all the Maida women to slake my lust with, why, by all that is holy, did it have to be with my best friend's fiancée's sister? What are the odds of that?* He marched straight into Tulon's dwelling.

"You don't look happy. Run into more of those Maida warrior-women you seem to love so much?" taunted Tulon, ushering out one of the many forest inhabitants that came to him so he could dispense justice.

Rusty was in no mood to be teased.

As the crowned Prince of the Forest, his friend's life had changed dramatically. And it was only going to get worse now with Rowena very pregnant. Not that Tulon seemed to mind. In fact, over the last few months, his friend had come into his own.

Rusty was proud of him—something he couldn't have said more than two years ago, when he'd learned that Tulon's clan had banished him. All that was ancient history. Tulon had been welcomed back to his clan with open arms and as much as Rusty knew it had been hard for his friend to mend the gap that existed between him and his mother's mate, Tulon had gone out of his way to do the right thing.

Tulon had also kept his promise to Rusty and re-introduced him to his sister. Things had gone well, but the spark he felt for her was dim compared to what had engulfed him with that Maida woman.

Thinking of her reminded Rusty why he was so mad to begin with.

"Tulon, there's something you should know," said Rusty now that they were alone.

"Have a drink first, my friend. I know I certainly need one," said Tulon, moving to an oak sideboard cabinet that housed the special homemade brew his kind drank.

He let Tulon pour him a glass of the special brew. He downed it in one large gulp.

"This must be something special you're about to tell me. You didn't even take the time to sniff the brew and list off the ingredients. So speak," said Tulon, motioning for him to sit.

Rusty preferred to stand. Before he could even begin, in barged the Maida woman. Her long chestnut brown hair trailed behind her, her sky-blue eyes were dark with fury and her lips were compressed into a tight line.

"There you are. I need you to take me home. Now!" she commanded, hands on her hips, legs braced like she was about to do battle.

"I take it *this* is what you wanted to talk about," said Tulon with a knowing smile.

Rusty growled low in his throat. "Yes," he snapped, trying hard not to pay any attention to the Maida woman. That was all but impossible. He could smell the heady scent of her sex as it swamped his senses. "Tulon, this is..."

"Tulon...this is my sister's mate," squeaked Tyrana, turning her head to get a good look at his friend.

Immediately, Tulon stood. Ever gracious, he rose and bowed to Rowena's sister. "It is indeed a pleasure to finally meet you. I've heard so much about you from Rowena that I feel as if I already know you."

Rusty watched as Mira...no, he corrected himself, Tyrana's eyes closed a fraction of an inch to form slits. He recognized that look.

"I highly doubt you know me at all. But none of this matters. I'm going home," she declared.

"Home? No, you must stay for the wedding. It will make Rowena so happy," said Tulon, trying to get Tyrana to sit.

Like Rusty, she preferred to stand.

"Look here, you..." Tyrana paused, as if sensing there was more to Tulon than met the eye. "I am going home now!" With that, she turned and marched out of Tulon's dwelling.

Rusty stood his ground as his friend's penetrating stare seared him.

"There's something you're not telling me," said Tulon, gently.

Rusty sighed. *This is going to be ugly.* "Okay, first I had no idea she was Rowena's sister. I thought she was simply a curious Maida woman. Anyway, she told me her name was Mira and then..." he coughed. "Well, then when she got lost in the Dark Forest things sort of escalated."

Tulon took a sip of his drink. "Escalated how?"

"Okay, I fucked her. There, are you happy?" snapped Rusty, moving to Tulon's cabinet to pour himself another much needed drink.

"And how was it?" asked Tulon.

"Best damn fuck I've ever had in my life," muttered Rusty before he knew he had spoken the words out loud. "Well, you know what I mean. It was good." He chuckled at his own admission.

There was a strange look in his friend's eyes Rusty didn't like. "I think there is something you are omitting," said his friend.

Rusty's eyes narrowed. *Did he read my mind? Can he even do that?* "Nope, that's it. I'm not into sharing the details. You know that, Tulon, shame on you."

His friend's laughter filled the dwelling. "If you think you can hide what you did from me, my friend, you are sadly mistaken. I'm not looking for details. I'm looking for honesty...and I think, Rusty, for that you will have to look deep within yourself," said Tulon, finishing his drink. "It doesn't matter. I know what's been done and it cannot be undone, and she cannot go home. Not now or ever. You will need to be the one to tell her that. Am I clear?"

Rusty bowed mockingly. "Sadly, yes. So I will take my leave of you and go find some chains, because that's what's going to be needed to keep that Maida woman here. Once she learns what we really are, she's going to quite literally lose her mind."

"Give yourself credit, Rusty. She's a strong Maida woman, like her sister. You will have to explain things to her gently but she might surprise you."

Rusty sensed there was more his friend wanted to share with him but at that moment, Rowena came back into the dwelling. Her eyes were puffy and immediately he knew she'd been crying.

Tulon rushed to her side. "There, there, *my love*...all will be okay. Tyrana will stay. I'm counting on Rusty to set things right. Everything will be as it should," said Tulon, wrapping his arms protectively around his mate. His eyes, though, had turned a cold grey. It was a look Rusty had come to recognize. Tulon expected him to do the impossible.

Rusty nodded and then exited, wanting to leave before Rowena fumed at him.

"Took you long enough," said Tyrana.

Rusty took a good look at her. She had one leg bent, braced against a nearby tree, giving him a splendid view of her legs. Her arms were crossed over her chest, pushing up her breasts. She looked as mad as a hellcat who had been denied a feast.

"Come with me," he said, leading the way to his dwelling on the other side of the Plains.

Rusty had made his home as far as possible from his warriors. He liked the simplicity and privacy of his place. *All that is about to be invaded.* He looked over his shoulder, pleased to see Tyrana following him.

When he reached his dwelling, he stopped. Like all the other dwellings, his home was round in structure. Unlike the rest, he had taken the time to add a sky portal so he could watch the stars at night from inside his dwelling. The thing he was the most proud of was the front and back gardens.

The front garden consisted of an array of exotic flowers while the back was where he grew all the vegetables. After training the warriors, he'd spend an hour in the front and then, after supper, another hour in the back garden. It helped calm his soul. Even after all the many battles he'd waged over the years and all the bloodshed, it was in his gardens where Rusty found peace and maybe a bit of redemption.

"This is beautiful," said Tyrana, gracefully moving into the flower garden.

He watched as she gently examined the flowers, her fingers skimming over the soft petals. "This must have taken you a lot of time."

There was genuine smile lighting up her face. *Wow, she likes my garden.* He had dreaded bringing her to his place but what choice did he have. He had marked her, changed her forever, yet she didn't know it yet. Sadly, all that was about to change. "You should see the back garden. That takes up most of my time these days," he said.

"Show me," she said.

He motioned for her to follow him around to the back. "After you, my lady," he said.

"Gentlemen first," she countered with a wink.

His heart lurched. A strange emotion twisted around deep inside of his subconscious. He tried hard to ignore it. "Here we are," he said, ushering her through the wide archway laced with wild ivy. As she passed him, he tried even harder to ignore the sway of her hips and the scent of wild lilies that streamed from her flowing hair.

"Oh my...this is breathtaking. Are those peas growing over there? And that looks like wild corn, lettuce, turnips, carrots, a row of *salama* beans, I just love those, and is that wild squash...how are you able to get them to grow? When I tried, they all died after taking root."

Her questions startled him. *Don't tell me she has a green thumb.*

Rusty moved to squat between the *salama* beans and the wild squash. "The *salama* beans help the wild squash to grow. It's a symbiotic relationship. Come here, you can see how the roots from the beans wrap themselves around the wild squash. The roots give off this obnoxious odor that deters insects from eating the wild squash."

He inhaled her unique perfume as she squatted beside him. "I never thought of that. That makes perfect sense. Will you show me how you got them to root in the first place? Every time I attempted it, they simply died," she admitted, reaching out to touch the large dark green leaves of the wild squash.

"I will do more than that. I will show you something very special." Before he could talk himself out of it, he grasped one of her hands in his and let the magic flow from him into her, letting her see the plants as he did. He heard her indrawn breath and felt her heart accelerate.

"This isn't possible," she said, awe lacing her sexy voice.

He knew what she saw. He was dusting the plants with love from Mother Earth and they were growing. Each plant's aura was outlined with a light gold glow. By wielding his magic, he forced the plants to accept his love and that nourished them, allowing them to grow.

Again Tyrana mumbled, "That's not possible."

He chuckled softly. "This and a lot more is possible, Tyrana, you only have to open your mind to the possibility of it."

She quickly withdrew her hand from his. "If I believed what I wished for were possible...I'd go crazy because it's not. It's not possible! Trust me, if there were a way, they'd have found it by now."

He watched her stand and compose herself—dismissing all that he had shown her. *Why can't things ever be simple*? Without a doubt, Rusty knew that in order for her to embrace the magic that lived within Mother Earth, she was first going to have to trust him and that was something one could only earn. He didn't like that at all.

"Take me home," she said, softly.

He stood beside her, wishing to draw her close. "I'm afraid that's impossible. I can't and won't take you home."

"Fine, I'll go on my own," she said, dismissing him and turning away from his body.

This time he didn't hesitate. He grabbed her and brought her body tight to his. "I'm afraid, my little filly, you can't go home ever again."

When she opened her mouth to protest, he lunged in and kissed her. She bit his lower lip. He chuckled but didn't stop kissing her. He felt her attempt to move her leg between his, which wouldn't do at all.

He hooked his leg around her foot and brought her to the ground. Using his weight, he settled on top of her waist, holding himself slightly off her. Rusty brought Tyrana's hands up around her head. The entire time, his tongue snaked in to plunder her mouth. She fought back with spunk and spice but it did no good.

He felt the moment when her fight turned into passion, when she opened to him, welcoming his actions. Immediately his cock bucked to attention. Rusty let go of her hands. Tyrana skimmed her tiny fingers through his wild hair. He shook with desire.

"I want you," she panted, breathing the words into his mouth.

Rusty moved to nibble her ear, trying to slow the tempo that was threatening to spiral out of control quickly. *Too quickly.* Already the tip of his cock was wet and he had to grit his teeth.

"What do you want?" he asked, licking the inside of her ear. Her shudder wrapped around him.

"I want your cock deep inside of me," she said, bucking her hips provocatively against him.

This was what he liked, a wild filly beneath him. What he didn't like were all the clothes they were wearing. Deciding to rely on instinct, he wielded the magic within him to vanquish their clothes. Tyrana's oomph of surprise was quieted when he moved his head to her already peaked nipple. His tongue laved first one nipple with attention and then the other. Her uninhibited sounds of pleasure spurred him on.

Rusty longed to plunge his cock deep within her wet core but he hesitated. Sitting back on his heels, he moved himself lower and used his shoulders to spread her legs wide. The sweetest honey he'd ever tasted was within reach. He stroked her swollen cleft, opening her folds slowly. She arched up onto her elbows to watch him work her. Her baby blue eyes were misty with sexual tension but he intended to play with her for a bit.

"Do you want me to lick you?" he asked, watching as heat surfaced to her chest. He loved how the areolas around her nipples were the shade of midnight rose, slightly brown and pink. He watched as she licked her lips and nodded.

"Pinch your nipples," he said, stroking her wet core with a deft finger. With her folds open, it was easy to find her already peaked nub of pleasure.

He watched as she stroked her breasts and then tweaked her nipples. Her head fell back in ecstasy and she moaned loudly, the sound rushing straight to his tight stones.

Rusty lowered his head to Tyrana's core and let his tongue take one long lap of her wetness. The taste of her sweet, musky sex rode straight to his core. He plunged his tongue into her opening and licked her roughly. His hands moved up to cup her ass and to leverage her opening up higher so he could plunge first one finger and then a second into her opening. Rusty's teeth grazed over her swollen nub, giving it a small nip. She arched fully into him, her legs grasping his head tight.

By the Saints, I could pleasure this woman until the end of days. The knowledge of that hit Rusty hard. He didn't ever want her to leave him. He didn't ever want her to fuck with another male. Rusty felt uneasy with the passion that ran through his body, soul and heart.

He felt her inner muscles clench around him and pulled back. Rusty didn't want her to climax yet. He needed to hear how much she wanted and needed him. If he had to use sex to make her see his way was the right way, well, so be it. Plus there was something she wasn't telling him—something she longed for that she'd built a wall around.

It was the one thing he had sensed when his magic had flowed into her. What that was he needed to know. There could be no more secrets between them. She was his. He had made her so. Now he had to make her believe in the impossible and open her heart to his.

She tugged on his hair, trying to get him back to where she ached the most. "Ahh, my little filly, not yet. Turn over," he growled.

Tyrana didn't hesitate. On her knees before him, she arched her back and her ass.

"You are so incredibly beautiful in your sexuality. Don't ever be afraid of it. But you've been a very naughty woman," he said, giving her ass a good smack which he followed with a quick kiss and small nip. "I'm going to teach you a little lesson," he said, smacking her other ass cheek. He watched as it turned pink and then he licked it.

He felt her battle. She liked what he was doing but she also liked to be the one in charge. "Submit to me. Put your head down on the ground and position your ass higher."

Tyrana hesitated for a few seconds and then complied. Rusty took his cock in his hands and stroked it hard. He fought not to spill his seed as he looked at this wonderful Maida woman who so openly embraced the sexual side of her nature. Rusty knew there was more to Tyrana than this.

As wild as she was when they mated, there was a softer side of her he longed to bring out. That's exactly what he planned on doing. First though, Rusty needed her to admit her want...her real ache...then he'd let the magic embrace her heart and soul.

"Like the view?" she asked saucily, bringing his attention back to her luscious body.

"You are only allowed to speak when you admit what you really want," he admonished as he ran a finger over each cheek and then let his tongue lick the crack of her ass. "Do you understand?"

Tyrana nodded, willing to play along.

Using his hands, he opened her cheeks and continued his sexual assault on her senses. Between long licks down her crack, he'd smack first one cheek and then the other, returning to lick and kiss it. She mewed her delight. Then he reached around to stroke her pebbled nub, tweaking it between two fingers as he continued to pay attention to her bottom. She tried again to arch into him.

He leaned his hard body over hers, letting his weight settle onto her raised ass. "What do you really want, Tyrana?"

"You," she rasped.

Rusty took his thick shaft in one hand and stroked it between her cheeks. She squirmed back more. "Yes, that's it, put it inside of me," she demanded.

He chuckled low. Tyrana was trying to take control of the situation and that wouldn't do at all. "No," he said, giving her nub a playful pat, adding to her ache as he moved his weight off her.

She twisted her head to look at him. Anger had replaced passion in her baby blues. "Put it inside of me," she snapped, sexually frustrated.

"No, Tyrana. Put your head back down to the ground. We will begin again," he said, abruptly moving off her prone body to stand. Rusty stroked his cock, letting her know how much he wanted her.

"You don't want me," she said, giving her ass a good shake.

"Head down, Tyrana, now, or I will leave you like this," he commanded

"You wouldn't," she said and then, thinking better of it, she did as instructed.

He knew she ached for sexual fulfillment, same as he did. By all that was holy, he longed more than anything to plunge in and ride her hard. But he had a job to do and he wasn't going to let his sexual need get in the way.

"Now I want you to play with your nub," he said, letting his weight settle onto her again so he could reach around to cup her breasts. He gave each nipple a painful tweak. He heard her indrawn breath.

He relaxed his weight and let her move an arm so she could play with herself, all the while keeping her head down. Then he moved back to her ass. This time he plunged one finger into the tight opening and with his other hand he placed two fingers into her wet pussy.

"Yes, that's it," she said.

Rusty withdrew both fingers. "No talking, Tyrana, until you tell me what you really want." When she understood that he wouldn't fulfill her sexually until she complied, only then did he repeat his actions.

Slowly he plunged one finger into her pussy and the other into her ass, letting both fill her. She squirmed back into his embrace.

"What do you really want, Tyrana?" he repeated.

"You," she said, panting with need.

Rusty withdrew a finger and smacked her ass and then leaned over her to kiss it. "No, Tyrana, what do you really want more than anything...what do you ache for always?" he asked, licking and kissing her back.

She shivered from his attentions. "I can't...please," she begged.

Rusty smacked her ass again, withdrawing a second finger from her core. He reached around, removed her hand that was playing with her nub and rubbed her wet mound.

"What do you really want, Tyrana? This is the last time I will ask," he said, still rubbing her mound, letting his hand slide through her slick opening.

He felt her shudder with need. He heard her indrawn breath as she fought her own inner battle to regain control of her emotions and her true desires.

"I want a baby!" she cried out with need.

Rusty caught the "what" that threatened to pass from his lips. *A baby? She wants a baby.* It all made sense. That's why she didn't want to see her sister or come to her wedding. *She wants what she thinks she can never have because of the Maida curse.*

Rowena had explained the fate of Maida women to him. She had told him that Tyrana was infertile. *So, my wild Tyrana is all really an act. She wants motherhood and because she can't have it, life holds no meaning for her.* The knowledge that his Tyrana ached for a baby slammed into him with primeval need.

He positioned his shaft at the tip of her cunt. He slid his cock a fraction of an inch into her, letting her body adjust to his thickness. "What if I said, Tyrana, that I can fulfill your want?" he breathed the words into her ear.

"What?" she asked, dazed with sexual passion.

He plunged his cock deep inside of her. "I'm..." he pulled out and then plunged back into her core. "Going to give you..." he pulled his cock out again and then drove in deeper, touching her womb, "what you want. And you are going to believe in magic." Then all sense left him as her inner muscles clenched around him, greedy with their need. Rusty rode her hard—swift, long strokes that left her breathless.

"Will you believe?" he asked, picking up his pace as he held her around her waist, pounding his desire into her.

"Yes, yes, anything. I'll believe anything, give it to me," Tyrana said, her sultry voice strained.

Rusty felt her tense and teeter on the edge of climaxing. He let his magic reach out to touch ever part of her body, heightening her pleasure. At the same time, Rusty used his magic to heal her barren womb and then and only then did he let her come. "That's it, my little filly, come for me, that's it..." he coaxed, letting his words wash over her.

He shortened his strokes, letting his cock ram into her as his stones bounced against her. Tyrana leaned forward onto the ground, heaving with desire as she came. She screamed his name as pleasure rode her hard, her muscles milking his shaft for his seed. He complied, letting his seed fill her, letting his seed do its magic.

Her head bowed down. Tyrana went limp. Sexually satisfied at last. Again using his magic, he cushioned her fall by conjuring up a soft blanket. She fell to it and only then did he finally withdraw from her core.

Tyrana turned over onto her back and reached for him. "That was the best fuck I've ever had," she said, a dazed smile spreading across her face.

"That's not all," said Rusty, gathering her tighter to him. "You're going to have a baby."

He watched as her eyes widened, disbelief and annoyance flaring to life. She moved out of his reach.

"Why would you do that, ruin a perfectly good after sex glow by saying that. I can't ever have a baby and I don't want to hear that word again."

She stood up and ran from him, naked and all.

That isn't the reaction I was hoping for. Rusty sighed wearily. Not sure what to do, he recalled how she'd been when he was a simple stallion and not a man. How she'd healed him with tenderness. He flashed into a stallion, hoping he was doing the right thing. *I will never understand females at all.*

Chapter Ten

Tyrana raced undeterred up the hill, across a river and into a forest of ferns. There were no trees so she didn't feel threatened. *Why would he say that? Why did he have to ruin the moment? I hate him.*

Thoughts spiraled through her mind of what she'd been through in the last few days with Rusty. Nothing made sense. Half the time she didn't understand what he was talking about—magic? *What is he, a wizard? There is no such thing as magic!*

If magic existed, she was sure her mother and aunts who ruled the Supreme High Fertility Council would know about it or, better yet, make it work for them. *Magic? The man is delusional.*

Tyrana liked her earlier assessment of him as being a rogue warrior. That was more rational and made a lot more sense than what happened to her around him. Take, for instance, her lack of clothing. Somehow, in the throes of passion, her clothing had simply disappeared. At the time it hadn't bothered her but now it did. Her feet were sore and she had a splinter in her right heel. Tyrana was at least thankful it was still sunny and warm.

She heard a familiar sound up ahead. Walking slowly, she made her way to the source. Nestled amongst tall ferns was her stallion—the magnificent wild creature she had spied in the Dark Forest. *Talk about a friend when you need it.*

She cautiously made her way to the beast. He turned his head to look at her. Again she had that familiar feeling there was more to this creature of the wild than met the eye. *Maybe it's his eyes. They remind me of Rusty. Ridiculous!*

Instead of reaching out to touch the wild stallion, she sat, overcome with grief. Tears streamed down and she gave in to the need to let it all out. She felt the stallion's movements as it made its way toward her. She didn't look up. Her shoulders shook as she blubbered away. The stallion nudged her shoulder. Her arms circled his neck, loving the feel of his soft, velvety smooth hair.

"I want to believe him, I really do. But life isn't like that. Life is cruel," she said, not expecting an answer. "More than anything, I want a baby but I can't. But if I let that hurt out...I can't function. The pain of it...the knowledge that my womb will never carry a baby is too much. Doesn't he see that's why I have to get home? I can't stay. I can't see Rowena again. It's too painful." Tyrana sobbed, feeling the warmth of the stallion as it flanked her.

He neighed and then, in a flash, she felt Rusty's muscular arms around her, gathering her to him.

"What?" she asked, startled into awareness. "You're the stallion? That's not possible." Tyrana attempted to wipe the tears from her face.

Rusty caught her hands and kissed her wet cheeks. The tenderness of his actions broke her heart in two. She fought to build a barrier around the barrage of emotions he evoked within her.

"Let it all out, Tyrana. I've got you. And I'm never letting you go," he said, whispering the words into her hair as he stroked her head, offering her his comfort when she needed it most.

"What just happened?" she asked, trying to rationalize one minute holding the stallion and then next being wrapped in Rusty's arms.

"I'm not a stallion. When you are ready, I will show you what I truly am," he said, rocking her gently. "What's more important is for you to understand that you are healed. In fact, you are more than healed. My seed has rooted with your egg and you are in the beginning stages of pregnancy."

She attempted to push him away. "Stop saying that. I can't handle it."

He tightened his grip on her. "Why won't you believe me?" he said, nuzzling her neck.

She hiccupped on a sob. "I can't. You're just a man, you can't really heal me."

She felt him release her, forcing her to stand. He moved away from her.

"I had hoped to give you more time to understand the magic of Mother Earth but I see you need to see things with your own eyes," said Rusty.

Then a blinding white light filled her vision and when next she blinked, gone was Rusty and in his place was a creature of myth and legend—a being that looked like it was half centaur and half Pegasus. He was beautiful to behold. Strong, muscular legs stood tall before her, his coat was a shiny rusty color while his upper torso was very much unchanged. It was the same muscular chest, same loving arms, same Rusty she knew. On his back, he had wide white wings which were outstretched behind him. His wings fanned the air.

He took a step toward her. "This is what I really am, Tyrana. I am called a Mage Pegcentaur and I am leader of the Mage Pegcentaur Clan," he said, giving her a courtly bow with one leg.

She shook her head, trying hard to make sense of it all. His words wove themselves into her subconscious.

"I've made you what I am. You're going to feel a slight burn as this is your first time, but I'm going to force the magic that is now running through your veins to change you."

She opened her mouth to protest but before she could, she felt the shift of muscle and bone. It was more than a slight burn. When next she looked she had four legs, the body of a horse, covered with a deep chestnut coat. Her upper torso was unchanged but on her back she felt the pull of the sky...of the air, beckoning to her. She careened her neck around and gawked. Two beautiful, large, white wings pulsed on her back as they buffeted the air. She moved shakily on her legs.

Instantly Rusty was beside her. "Get a feel for your legs, my little filly, before you take to the air," he said, letting his hands roam over her coat.

She sighed. The intense pleasure of his fingers stroking her...it was indescribable. "How is this possible?"

"Magic is all around you but we are of the old magic—the foundation that formed Mother Earth. I've given you a part of my essence to force the magic to work within you. And the best part of it, Tyrana, is that you really are pregnant. Let your senses reach out to feel what's taking place within your womb," he said, running his hands over her coat the entire time, coaxing her to relax, letting the magic flow from him into her.

Tyrana did as instructed. She closed her eyes and within a second she sensed the change within her body. "What? I can't believe it," she cried, tears falling down her cheeks.

"I thought this was supposed to make you happy," said Rusty, moving to her front to embrace her in a hug.

"Why would you do this to me? You don't even know me." Tyrana sighed. She was tired, completely bewildered and a bit afraid she was losing her mind.

"I may not know all of you yet but I certainly plan to. Trust me, this was the last thing I expected but don't think for one second I'm not happy," he said. "Will you walk with me?"

Walk? I can barely stand on these legs. "I'm not sure I can."

"You will. Follow my lead," he said, reaching out to take her hand.

She shivered from his touch. She looked down. Her breasts were larger than before and her nipples had puckered into tight buds.

"I had no idea you would look so incredibly beautiful. You have no idea how much I want you," he said, flanking his body next to hers.

Tyrana bit her lip. She was concentrating on moving her legs. They were still shaky but she was proud to still be standing and walking. All of a sudden, she felt the ground shake.

She turned her head and gawked. Hundreds of creatures like Rusty were galloping straight toward them. Leading them was a creature who caused her breath to hitch. It was a black unicorn. He was breathtakingly beautiful, yet terrifying at the same time.

"Don't run," whispered Rusty.

The man is nuts. I couldn't run with these legs if my life depended on it. I certainly hope it doesn't depend on it. Even as she thought that, she also fought with her wings, which were beating faster. She felt her heart accelerate as her body tried to soar into the air. The thought terrified her.

"Take a calming breath. I won't leave you. You have nothing to be worried about." Rusty turned around and faced the group.

A blinding white light filled her vision and when next Tyrana looked, instead of the unicorn stood Tulon, her sister's soon-to-be husband. "What?" she asked, mystified.

"I am pleased, my friend. You did the right thing. She is beautiful," said Tulon, nodding his head toward Tyrana.

Tyrana felt the urge to position her body behind Rusty's. She didn't like everyone looking at her. It left her feeling exposed and vulnerable. Sensing her discomfort, Rusty flashed her back into her human form, equipped with her original clothing. She smiled shyly up at him.

"Thank you," she said.

"You're welcome. From now on, it is my job to see to your pleasure," he declared.

Then he reared up on his hind legs, his wings stretched out more and he soared into the air. His voice was a low rumble vibrating over the land. "My fellow Mage Pegcentaurs, I give you my mate, Tyrana."

Mate? Tyrana swallowed. She wasn't sure about that.

"Very soon we will bring forth the new lives within her and we will all further rejoice," said Rusty, quickly coming to land beside her.

He flashed into human form and hugged her. She didn't fight his embrace. Instead, she yielded to his strength. Then his words washed over her but before she could ask more, her sister materialized next to her.

"Tyrana, I am so happy for you. You don't know how much I longed to tell you the truth," said Rowena, rubbing her large belly.

Tyrana watched her actions. Instead of feeling rage and injustice, she felt a sense of camaraderie. "What are you?"

Her sister giggled. Tulon actually laughed. "She is a Centaur and my mate. I am Tulon, the Prince of the Forest. You, Tyrana, are mate to my best friend, Rusty, Leader of the Mage Pegcentaurs."

Chapter Eleven

Tyrana giggled. "If only Mother could see us now."

"I am not sure Mother will ever be ready for the truth," admitted her sister. "Ahh, Ty, feel this. Talk about a kicker," said Rowena, reaching for her hand.

Tyrana let her sister take her hand to pull it to Rowena's round belly. She stilled in anticipation. She felt the baby within her sister's womb kick her hand hard. She grinned. Warmth radiated through her. "That felt wonderful."

"Wish I did," declared Rowena, rubbing her back.

Instantly, Tulon had her cradled in his arms like she weighed nothing at all. "Put me down."

"Your back is hurting you and your time is soon. I have no intention of putting you down until I have you safe in our bed, my love," he said, kissing her soundly on the lips to quiet her.

Tyrana gasped. "What do you mean her time is soon?"

Rowena playfully smacked Tulon's arms. "I don't think so, Ty. He's just being his overbearing self. I'm sure I have many more months to go. It's only been three months."

"What is it with these Maida women," said Rusty, placing his hands on his hips.

"I tried to explain things to her, Rusty, but she keeps insisting it won't happen soon," huffed Tulon, looking exasperated.

"Well, how long is it?" asked Tyrana, trying to make sense of what they were implying.

"Time? It has nothing to do with days or months...it has to do with the maturity of the magic that grows within her womb. She is carrying a child that will be part unicorn, part Centaur and filled with magic. Trust me, her time is soon," declared Tulon. "Now, if you will excuse us."

With that Tyrana watched as Tulon marched off, carrying her still laughing sister in his arms.

"I really don't understand that. What did you mean when you said we'd rejoice for the lives within me?" asked Tyrana, turning her attention to Rusty. There was a glint of mischievousness in his eyes that sparked her interest. "What?"

"Reach out with your senses again to your womb," he said, flashing back into a Mage Pegcentaur, looking mighty proud of himself.

Showoff. She did as instructed and stilled. "Two heartbeats? I sense two heartbeats? Does that mean—"

"Twins. Yes," he said. "Come fly with me."

She shook her head. Her mind was still grappling with the news that she was carrying twins and now he wanted her to fly with him. *The man is nuts. Crazed beyond belief.*

She smiled. And for once in her life, that smile reached deep within her soul. It felt wonderful...like an aphrodisiac. Her laugh bubbled unheeded as she felt the slight brush of his power reach her. Instantaneously she flashed into a Pegcentaur. Her wings once again buffeted the air around her. She kicked her legs and attempted to run from him.

"I said come fly with me." This time there was no mistaking the command in his voice.

She ran harder, finally finding her pace as her legs flew underneath her without thought. Too bad her wings wouldn't listen to her. She felt them beating faster as she ran and once she swore her feet had actually stopped touching the ground.

"You understand I can make you fly with me? Nothing will harm you. Ever," said Rusty, his voice a seductive rumble as he flew within a wing beat of her.

She laughed again, loving the freedom he evoked within her. "You promise?" she asked, still slightly afraid of this magical unknown world she had found herself tossed into.

"With my heart and soul."

She reached for his outstretched hand, her wings seemingly knowing when to beat stronger and faster as he pulled her up toward him—in the air. The warm breeze rushed across her senses. She felt euphoric.

"Let your wings guide you, not your legs," said Rusty, never once letting go of her hand.

For that Tyrana was thankful. She gave his hand a slight squeeze and immediately felt his growl of approval. Together they flew up higher through the white, fluffy clouds.

"This is amazing. I never thought... Rusty, I can see the land below me. It is so beautiful."

"Yes, it is. Amazing, isn't it? The things we take for granted are the most precious things in our life," he answered, bringing his body closer to hers.

It dawned on Tyrana then that there was more to this man...this Mage Pegcentaur, than he showed to others. There was a side to him that was quiet and reflective, and from what she had seen in his gardens, he loved to nourish things to life.

"You don't really want to be their leader, do you?" she asked, letting him guide her to a high mountain cliff. Her legs landed a bit unevenly, but like always, he was there to steady her, to provide her with comfort. And she let him. Tyrana let this man who had changed her life so much wield his magic on her. And more importantly, Tyrana realized this man loved her for who she was, not what she had been. And she loved him for that.

"When the time comes, a new leader will step forward, but until that time I will do my duty."

"Is that what I am to you, a duty?" She gulped, hating that she had to ask.

He flashed them both back into human form.

"I think you forgot something," said Tyrana, her body naked, shivering from the cold.

"No, I don't think I did."

She watched as he created a fleece blanket and wrapped it around himself. Feeling peeved, she huffed, her breath steaming in the cold air.

"So you're going to let me freeze to death just because I asked a question you didn't like."

"You are my mate. Of course you are my duty, but you are much more than that. I need for you to understand that your old ways are gone for good," he declared. "Now lie down."

Rusty watched as Tyrana arched her eyebrows sharply together. It was a look he was becoming accustomed to. She was annoyed with him. *Well, so what. She has to learn she's my other half and what better way than to show her.*

"You understand that you are mine forever. You understand that you can never go home," he said, watching as she placed her hands over her breasts in an attempt to warm them. "Now lie down and spread your legs for me."

"No," she replied.

He knew she was completely unaware that her magic was reaching out around her. Sparks practically flew around her. He needed her to learn how to harness the magic that ran in her veins. He also knew he was playing with fire.

"I will make you lie down and spread your legs for me," he said, his voice hard and edgy.

She cocked her eyebrow higher at him. "Ohh, I so don't think you will. Hey, I'm no longer cold," she said, her body flush with warmth.

Rusty couldn't help himself. He laughed.

"What's so funny?" she asked, her face heating with warmth.

"Sorry, Tyrana. I'm trying to teach you how to harness your magic and the use of emotions is the most productive way. I thought if I got you mad, you would heat up." He reached for her.

She stepped back, a little too close to the cliff for his liking. He stilled.

"So that was a test."

He nodded.

"So let me get this straight. I can actually regulate my own body temperature by willing it to be."

Again he nodded.

"Still, you never did answer my initial question. Am I just another duty to you, Rusty?"

He moved forward so fast she didn't have a chance to escape. He cupped her face in his large hands. "You are the love of my life." He breathed the words into her open astonished mouth and kissed her hard, claiming all that was his.

Tyrana returned his kiss and then she arched her head back. "You have made me complete like I never thought I could be. I don't ever want to go home again but we will be adding on to your home," she said, giving his lip a playful nip. "You won't be needing this."

Rusty let her move the fleece blanket off him. When she reached down to cup his large stones, he all but bounced on his feet. She squeezed them gently. He gritted his teeth as desire fired through his system.

"So you're okay with the fact that I'm not Maida," he said, trying to quench the mad rush that overtook his passion, the part of him that wanted to force Tyrana into a submissive pose.

She didn't answer. Instead she inched her mouth lower to what she really wanted to kiss—his long, thick cock. She gently grasped it with one hand and then licked the tip of it. He shivered.

"I don't care what you are but there is one other thing I'm going to want you to do," she said, placing the tip of his wet shaft in her mouth. She sucked hard, even as he tried to move it out of her mouth.

"And that would be..." Rusty was amazed he could actually talk. The feeling of his cock lodged in her warm, inviting mouth was so overwhelming it was taking a lot of control to not simply pump his seed deep down her throat.

"Let me suck you," she demanded, cupping his heavy stones in her hand as her other finger played with the crack of his ass. His head tilted back as he growled.

"Say it," she sighed, opening her mouth wider to force his thick cock down her throat.

He grabbed her hair but kept still, letting her get used to the feel of him. Her tongue circled and licked his thick column as she sucked on him.

"Say it," she repeated, moving his shaft from her mouth to hold in her hand.

Rusty looked down. The sight was so erotic he trembled with need, passion and a fierce protectiveness for the lovely Maida woman who he knew he would always love tenderly no matter how rough their love play got. She needed tenderness as much as she needed control.

"Suck it," he said, growling as she complied.

The muscles in his legs strained as need fueled through him. He tried to stop bucking but she grasped his ass, then her hand worked his engorged member, stroking him as her mouth sucked him. It was too much for him. "I'm going to—"

"Do it," she mumbled, cupping his tight stones.

She squeezed them hard and Rusty roared as his seed fought for release. He bucked faster against her, loving how she kept up the pressure at the base of his cock while her warm mouth sucked hard on his long column. Finally he let her have it. She drew him in deep as his seed filled her. He tried to draw out but she continued to lavish and lick it clean.

His entire body shook and his stones sagged with relief. "That was incredible. I had no idea." He breathed deeply, letting her know just how much her actions had meant to him.

"I know," she said, kissing him.

He tasted his own passion on her lips as he darted a finger between her legs to her wet pussy.

"So wet, my little filly. It's my turn," he said, lowering them both to the ground. Using his magic, he created a dozen puffy blankets to buffer their bodies. "Now spread your legs for me."

"With pleasure," she replied, a sexy flirtatious smile lighting up her charming face.

"Trust me, the pleasure is all mine."

With that, Rusty set about ensuring Tyrana knew all about the art of pleasuring. Using his mouth, he made her climax three times before he brought her limp body tight to his, sliding his still hard cock into her swollen core.

"Love me tender," breathed Tyrana, slightly exhausted from her orgasms but still wanting all he could give her.

"Always, my little filly. Always," declared Rusty.

Renee Field can be reached at www.reneefield.com[1]

When not writing, Renee is promoting other authors on StoryFinds.com, a site she founded in 2012 to help support Indie authors.

Renee loves to write a variety of genres. She writes erotic romance for Ellora's Cave, & HQN Spice Briefs and sensual paranormal romance as an Indie author. Field also writes nitty gritty young adult and paranormal young adult romance novels under the pen name Renee Pace (www.reneepace.com).

Renee calls Halifax, Nova Scotia, Canada home and loves her view of the Atlantic Ocean. She is a member of Romance Writers' of America, and her local Romance Writers of Atlantic Canada. She juggles work, four children and is a firm believer in soul-mates and the power of the sea.

Renee loves to hear from fans.

Follow her on Facebook at https://www.facebook.com/ReneeFieldRomanceAuthor

Twitter @pararomance

Email: renee@reneefield.com

Renee is also the Founder of StoryFinds.com[2] – a site geared to promote Indie and award winning ebooks.

Titan Series:

Rapture, **Titan series Book 1** http://www.barnesandnoble.com/w/rapture-renee-field/1012416444?ean=2940148270706

Bliss, **Titan series Book 2** http://www.barnesandnoble.com/w/bliss-renee-field/1119123634?ean=2940151670814

Erotic Romance Siren series:

1. http://www.reneefield.com
2. http://www.storyfinds.com/

Claiming the Temptress (erotic novella) (HQN Spice Briefs) http://www.barnesandnoble.com/w/ claiming-the-temptress-renee-field/ 1111929372?ean=9781459242272

Claiming Poseidon's Heart (erotic romance) http://www.barnesandnoble.com/w/ claiming-poseidons-heart-renee-field/ 1118745700?ean=2940149563135

Claiming A Siren's Heart (erotic romance) http://www.barnesandnoble.com/w/ claiming-a-sirens-heart-renee-field/ 1118745689?ean=2940149563005

What to Read After FSOG: The Gemstone Collection (WTRAFSOG Book 7) http://www.barnesandnoble.com/w/ what-to-read-after-fsog-lexi-buchanan/ 1120630351?ean=2940150351899

Sweet and Spicy Spells (paranormal erotic romance novel) - http://www.barnesandnoble.com/w/ sweet-and-spicy-spells-christine-dabo/ 1100322147?ean=9781419913846

Spice Me Up (contemporary erotic romance) http://www.barnesandnoble.com/w/spice-me-up-renee-field/ 1120389974?ean=9781419991455

<u>Darklander Lovers Series (erotic paranormal romance)</u>

Be My Vampire Tonight (Darklander Lovers, Book One) http://www.barnesandnoble.com/w/be-my-vampire-tonight-renee-field/ 1024640553?ean=9781419927355

Be My Werecat Tonight (Darklander Lovers, Book Two) http://www.barnesandnoble.com/w/be-my-werecat-tonight-renee-field/ 1025775146?ean=9781419927683

Be My Warlock Tonight (Darklander Lovers, Book Three)
http://www.barnesandnoble.com/w/be-my-warlock-tonight-renee-field/
1027179760?ean=9781419927799

Contemporary Romance:

Embrace (sweet contemporary romance novella)
http://www.barnesandnoble.com/w/embrace-renee-field/
1118730257?ean=2940148290711

Bake, Love, Write: 105 Authors Share Dessert Recipes and Advice on Love and Writing - http://www.barnesandnoble.com/w/
bake-love-write-lois-winston/1120365873?ean=9781940795133

Don't miss out!

Visit the website below and you can sign up to receive emails whenever Renee Field publishes a new book. There's no charge and no obligation.

https://books2read.com/r/B-A-HRN-AEIG

BOOKS 2 READ

Connecting independent readers to independent writers.

Did you love *Love Me Tender*? Then you should read *Be My Vampire Tonight*[3] by Renee Field!

Bidding on a masked man at an auction is all for a good cause, but what happens when he turns out to be a vampire who has the power to unleash the wild woman lying dormant inside you?

As a Darklander vampire, Mitch has spent a century living in a bleak world, but all that changes when he sees Tina. The beast living within Mitch wants to stake his claim. Mitch knows taking Tina's virginity will change her forever, but try explaining that to a woman whose passion cannot be denied.

Tina holds the key to his freedom, but Mitch will be damned forever before he turns her over as a slave for his master.

Book one in the Darklander Lovers series.

3. https://books2read.com/u/3RoMDG

4. https://books2read.com/u/3RoMDG

Read more at www.reneefield.com.

Also by Renee Field

A Warriors of Maida Novella
Love Me Wild
Love Me Tender
Love Me Strong
Love Me Wild

Darklander Lovers
Be My Warlock Tonight
Be My Vampire Tonight
Be My Werecat Tonight

Elemental Love
Heart of Mine

Riverton Cove series
Embrace

Titan series
Rapture
Bliss

Standalone
Claiming A Siren's Heart
Claiming Poseidon's Heart
A Siren's Wish
Fairy Cursed
Summer Heat
Queen of Dragons
Summer Heat
Electrify Me

Watch for more at www.reneefield.com.

About the Author

Renee loves to write a variety of genres. She writes for HQN Spice Briefs and also writes sensual paranormal romance, and contemporary romance as an Indie author. Field also writes nitty gritty young adult and paranormal young adult romance novels under the pen name Renee Pace. Renee calls Halifax, Nova Scotia, Canada home and loves her view of the Atlantic Ocean. She is a member of Romance Writers' of America, and her local Romance Writers of Atlantic Canada. She juggles work, four children and is a firm believer in soul-mates and the power of the sea.

Renee loves to hear from fans. She can be reached by email at reneefieldauthor@gmail.com

Read more at www.reneefield.com.

www.ingramcontent.com/pod-product-compliance
Lightning Source LLC
Chambersburg PA
CBHW051248180626
46816CB00004BA/1388